The End of Free Love

The End of Free Love

Susan Steinberg

FC2
Normal/Tallahassee

Published by FC2 with support provided by Florida State
University, the Unit for Contemporary Literature of the
Department of English at Illinois State University, the Program
for Writers of the Department of English of the University of Illi-
nois at Chicago, the Illinois Arts Council, and the Florida Arts
Council of the Florida Division of Cultural Affairs

Address all inquiries to: Fiction Collective Two, Florida State University, c/o English Department, Tallahassee, FL 32306-1580

ISBN: Paper, 1-57366-106-6

Library of Congress Cataloging-in-Publication Data
Steinberg, Susan.
  The end of free love / by Susan Steinberg.—1st ed.
    p. cm.
  ISBN 1-57366-106-6
1. Domestic fiction, American. 2. Jewish families—Fiction.
3. Jewish women—Fiction. I. Title.
PS3619.T4762 E53 2003
813'.6--dc21
                                        2002009562

Cover Design: Victor Mingovits
Book Design: Tara Reeser

Produced and printed in the United States of America
Printed on recycled paper with soy ink

This program is
partially supported
by a grant from the
Illinois Arts Council

ACKNOWLEDGMENTS

Several stories from this collection first appeared elsewhere in various forms.

"Isla" appeared in *The Gettysburg Review*.

"Nothing" appeared in *Quarterly West*.

"Saturday" appeared in *Quarterly West*.

"testing," appeared in *New Letters*.

"Away!" appeared in *Berkeley Fiction Review*.

"The End of Free Love" appeared in *The Cream City Review*.

"Forward" appeared in *Indiana Review*.

"Far" appeared in *Other Voices*.

"Winner" appeared in *Confrontation*.

"There's a window." appeared in *LIT*.

"Stay with me." appeared in *The Massachusetts Review*.

"Standstill" appeared in *Boulevard*.

"Start" appeared in *Ascent*.

"Trees" appeared in *Northwest Review*.

"Opening" appeared as "Loose" in *slope.org*.

I wish to thank John Edgar Wideman, Noy Holland, John Clayton, Stephen Clingman, Lynne Layton, Nicholas Montemarano, K. R. Mogensen, and the University of Massachusetts, Amherst.

CONTENTS

ONE

Isla

1. Never tuck the napkin.

2. Four stars means tops. One two three four. Meaning the top. Número uno.

3. Spread the napkin like this. A flick and drop. Do it. These are real cloth. A flick. Drop in the lap.

4. Tell the waitress your drink. Tea please por favor and bread.

5. Always ask for by the window. For the sunset.

6. Sugar is the enemy. It gets in the blood and spreads. We all get it from the sugar. Our one enemy number one is sweets.

7.   Trust me. They aren't Jews. There by the kitchen. Don't look.

8.   White sand is all you need. Setting sun. What more could you need?

9.   Salt slows the blood. It poisons. Take a glass of water. Pour in a shaker of salt. Now two. The blood from salt.

10. Never buy German made.

11. Seabirds are dirty and beggars.

12. An aperitif. Rouge. A twist.

13. They work the native girls hard. These girls are close to your age. They make a nickel an hour. Just nickels in a four star. How would you survive? This is why we tip. We're known for good tipping.

14. Hard liquor is the enemy. It poisons the bloodstream. Hard liquor is for the crass. The whiskies and gins. They can have it.

15. There are things your old pop knows.

16. Never gamble.

17. Never smoke.

18. Sometimes we cheat.

19. Red sunsets are all you need. See the sailboats? A picture postcard. When have you seen a red sunset? Think. Never. I like the blue boat there but sailboats tip. One tilt and splash.

20. New Yorkers are crass. Look at that fellow eating. By the kitchen. What a piece of meat. Look. Showy. An animal from New York you know it. That slob. Napkin tucked. He's hard from the city living don't I know it.

21. Aperitifs come rouge and blonde. Some ice and a twist of lemon and you sip. Aperitifs come first before dinner. With a twist. Sip slow. After dinner drinks come after.

22. When you want more tea. Cuando quieres más tea. Say, more tea. Dices, más tea por favor.

23. The waitress thinks you're my girlfriend.

24. Blonde. Ice and a twist.

25. They make nickels an hour. They have children at home. They live in shanties in ghettoes. How would you survive? They start when they're thirteen. No car no trips. No Sunday school. Some start at twelve.

26. Never bring home a New Yorker. You'll kill me. Never bring home a non-Jew.

27. A trip for my girl and we deserve it don't we Sweetie?

28. Never feed the seabirds. They carry sickness. They eat garbage from the ghettoes. Let the slobs bring them bread.

29. You can tell non-Jews. Even dark-haired ones. The small handbags. Plastic beads. Fake stones.

30. I can still get a young girl.

31. Four stars means tops. Not three but four. Straighten. Look proud. Four stars Sweetie. Wait until your mother hears. Her head will go through the roof.

32. Never sit by the kitchen. You don't want to hear it. The clatter. Or see it.

33. Never go to the ghetto.

34. We'll start with this. Soup. Then this. Ensalada.

How old are you? I guess seventeen. Am I right? Seventeen. Sweetie what do you think? How old is she? Wipe your face. She must be seventeen. This here's my girlfriend. You laugh. This is my lucky lady. Say hello Sweetie. Say hola to the waitress. Hola Sweetie. I want this here and my lucky girlfriend will have this and done well-done. And bring me a clean knife.

35. First blow on the spoon.

36. If it's too hot add ice.

37. New Yorkers are showy. They drive German cars. You know this.

38. Playing slots is not gambling. Five dollars big deal. Nickels.

39. Place the knife on the plate. All the way top and bottom against the rim. Not like this but like this. It shouldn't touch the table.

40. Never ride a sailboat. One tip then splash and you drown. Would you like to drown? Would you? You don't want to find out. Trust me.

41. Leave a bite on your plate.

42. We can fool the waitress. She's staring. Look. I'll put my arm around you. Sit still. Don't look she's looking. We're so bad.

43. Jews don't drink beer with dinner. They don't drink milk. They don't drink hard liquor. We don't have the stomachs. Besides.

44. No one drinks the native coffee. It will put you under the table. You could stand a knife up in their coffee.

45. Taste before salting. Always. Why presume? Your mother the way she shakes the salt. She salts meat.

Soup. Foods salted. Am I right? She would salt a cake if you didn't take the shaker. Her blood will screech to a halt. I always told her. Watch it.

46. You're the tops.

47. Jews don't call dinner supper.

48. If you laugh then laugh quiet.

49. New Yorkers are slobs. Look tugging on his meat. Crass. A zoo animal.

50. Cut three squares of meat. Then eat them one two three. Then cut three more. Then eat one two three.

51. Your eyes are bigger than your stomach.

52. You need fat on the skeleton. Why don't you eat up? You would never survive a roundup. Do you know what a roundup is? What do they teach in that slob Sunday school? You need some fat.

53. If it turned cold send it back.

54. Blondes are lookers. The New Yorker's date. Mean looking but a blonde. That my Sweetie is a looker. By the kitchen. Your mother was a looker a long way back.

55. You don't eat the garnish.

56. Cut smaller pieces. Do you want to choke?

57. We can't go into the ghetto. We can drive around the edge. I can show you how the other half survives. Would you like that Sweetie? They carry pistols and knives. They sell their trinkets. We don't need that garbage. And the poor children. We'll keep our doors locked.

58. Un vaso de vino. For my young lady. White or red? Wait don't tell me. Blanco o rojo? Am I right?

Blanco or rojo Sweetie? How about it? She's shy and always has been. She can sip some blanco. Her mother's head will shoot to the stars. Her first glass.

59. Solamente cuando su madre no está aquí. Comprendes?

60. Your pop takes care. This ring will be yours. Solid fourteen. This is fashion. Not a trinket. Your mother chose the stone and one day my sweets. All for you. But what's the hurry am I right?

61. The world is unfair. A looker and a slob. Turn slowly and tell me. The blonde with the. Tell me is she a looker? Mean looking with the cigarette. The lipstick. Now look. Am I right? Don't look.

62. If you can't pay you wash dishes.

63. The middle of the island is a zoo. Pistol shooting. Stray goats. They shoot dogs and live in shanties. They live in ghettoes. Such litter. They race cars.

64. I'll never let you starve.

65. There are things we do when no one's looking. Everyone does. Your old pop isn't so bad. There are just things that happen. You understand this Sweetie. Things. Comprendes for me por favor.

66. We all used to struggle. We ate soup from cans. Before you Sweetie. Before we left the zoo. But we danced. We went dancing. But soups from cans imagine can you?

67. Let's be extravagant.

68. Tap the water glass for attention. Ting ting. Or raise one finger like this.

69. American coffee por favor black no sugar. Más tea for my lady.

70. Eat up. You're a skeleton. Skin on a skeleton. Don't you like dinner? This isn't a joke. Eat up. Let's see you eat. Is it any good? Chew first then swallow. Slow. This isn't a race.

71. German cars are the enemy. Do you know this? Do you know why? What do they teach you on Sundays? Peace and love? The happy world? To hell. Ask me about the car seats. Come on Sweetie. Ask me about the ghettoes.

72. There are things your old pop knows.

73. Dessert is for slobs. The sugar is what kills. The sugar got all your grandparents. All your aunts and uncles. That and the smoking. The drinking. All of them. Ask your mother and still she eats desserts. She pours the salt. She smokes and drinks. Did you know this? She keeps it quiet. You didn't know.

74. The waitress thinks I'm twenty years younger.

75. The waitress never went to school. Imagine no school Sweetie.

76. There is always someone better smarter funnier. Always someone richer happier better. Always someone nipping at your seat. Shoving you out. Tell your poor mother. She never listened. You have to watch it or you'll fall. I warned her. She was in fashion. I got a fat wallet. They colored her hair. Fatter and they painted her nails. Magic. How she looked on our honeymoon. But now? Shape up I told her. Someone will push you out. Did she listen? Eat Sweetie. Watch it I told her. Does she listen?

77. The waitress is no older than seventeen. She's closer to your age. You're close to seventeen hard to believe. You're fourteen hard to believe.

78. Your pop's a strong man. Look at the size of this fist. Let's see your little hand Sweetie. Make a fist. I could crush that little thing.

79. I'll never let you get hurt.

80. They grow up quick here. They know how to make a man happy. They cook can they ever. Rice and beans and meat from their farms. Imagine a farm of stupid skinny goats Sweetie. Would you eat goat? They eat the meat and boy can they clean a house. They treat men as men. The boss of the house. They work as maids. Waitresses. They know when enough's enough. They know how to give. How to listen. How to milk a goat. And they keep quiet.

81. Chew then swallow. There's no race.

82. You can always send it back.

83. Watch your old pop in action. Come here honey. Ting. Ting. An after dinner por favor. Surprise me.

84. I'm the boss. Do you hear me? I can always disown you.

85. You never can win.

86. Sometimes we lie.

87. Obesity is a crime that poor slob. He should be dragged out and shot. I'll hold a pistol. You grab the steak knife. Cut off his fingers. He'll still eat poor slob. We can take his date and drive and drive until they find us.

88. Never drive German made.

89. I was an expert dancer way back. Ask your mother.

90. Breathe the air. It's the real thing. Salt air. Sun. You can taste it in the air.

91. You're my lucky lady. My Sweetie. Say hola to the waitress. My girl here's a good girl. She goes to school. Not a brain though. You know what a brain is? She's not the brainy type. Cómo se dice? Who knows right? But she'll make me proud. I have plans for this one. I have a business. I'm el presidente. She'll learn the ropes. Just a joke. She's not good with business. Easy. Where's your humor? A joke Sweetie. Joking.

92. You're number one.

93. Say, dónde está el cuarto de baño?

94. No dessert. I'm watching it. How about you Sweetie? Do you dare? Some cake? Pie? Look at those eyes. Her eyes are bigger than her stomach. Look at her looking but I think she knows better.

95. I love you Sweetie.

96. Picture the ghettoes. Shanties. Little shack houses. Hardly a window. Goats chewing the dried up grass. Thin dirt roads. Cars racing past. They race into children. We're so lucky. Guess what else. They toss children from roofs. The accidents.

97. The only good German is a what Sweetie? The only good German is a what German? Come on Sweetie.

98. You're a lucky thing.

99. You're Jewish first. American second. German last.

100. The slots age is eighteen. I'll give you five dollars. All those nickels. Your mother's head will hit the ceiling. We won't tell her. She used to be different way back. She was some looker. You don't remember. This was in New York. She could dance. We danced like a couple of kids.

101. American coffee. You can always tell American.

102. The salt air clears the head. Don't worry about your mother. She'll snap back. I did nothing wrong. We'll send a postcard. I did nothing at all. She can't say I did. What has she said? She can't say anything. I warned her. You can't listen to her.

103. You wave away musicians like this. A flick of the wrist. They're a pain in the seat. They play for tips. Beggars.

104. Never bring home a musician.

105. We can make you eighteen. Some lipstick. Magic. Four years older. You'll be my girlfriend. We'll dance.

106. I should never have married your mother.

107. The sky's the limit. How about that Sweetie? How about we get you in fashion? New shoes Sweetie. The ones they wear now. The ones they wear here. Tops. Lipsticks. You'll come back a new you. Your mother will die from shock. We'll get you a hairdo. New nails. The sun's the limit.

108. The Germans are the enemy. They got your great grandparents.

109. You die you rot.

110. I always told her no children. She was too young. And why did I need children? She should have never. She wasn't ready. Accidents happen. But did she listen? Does she ever?

111. It's good to get away. You leave everything behind. But it catches you Sweetie. I hate to say it. But it nips you in the seat.

112. Never ask me why.

113. You pour a dot of cream. Wait. Another dot. Wait. See how it lightens? If you pour too much you mess the whole cup. I mean do you want coffee or a glass of milk? Ask yourself.

114. I deserve the best don't I? She couldn't give the best. She gave half that. A quarter that. This fat wallet and she gave nothing. Don't I deserve the most?

115. Guess the check. Hurry Sweetie. Guess it. A hint. Think high. Higher. Higher. You'll never guess. Never.

116. Don't stare. Look at them stumbling out. Poor slobs.

117. A nice Jew is all you need. A nice home. I'll fill your wallet. You don't need your mother. You don't need school. Finish junior high if you like. Find a nice Jew. A nice house. Take an island honeymoon.

118. Don't listen to your mother.

119. You're Jewish first. American second. German last.

120. Your mother never loved her child.

121. You're my número uno.

122. Wipe your face.

123. Take the check. You're paying. You're my lucky girlfriend right? Dinner's on you. Come on Sweetie. Where's your wallet? Show the waitress your fat wallet. Who's going to pay if not you? There are dishes waiting. Come on Sweetie. We're waiting for you. Come on. Waiting.

124. A joke. Just a joke. Where's your humor? Both of you.

125. Put the napkin on your plate.

126. You are your own worst enemy.

127. A five-dollar tip can buy a new goat.

128. A trip just you and me. It's been fun hasn't it? We'll get you in fashion. Then we can see some of that white sand and look for shells. We can lie around the sand like a couple of kids. How about it Sweetie? We'll race past the ghetto. I have friends in there. Would you eat goat? We can race through the ghetto and see what's what.

129. How about it Sweetie? Let's do this again sometime. While we still can.

130. I love you Sweetie. How about that?

131. Wipe here Sweetie. Wipe your eyes.

132. Give me the napkin. Let me help.

133. How can I help?

134. How can I help Sweetie?

Nothing

There's one: music. Then two is comics and three foods.

(In music there's more as in lyrics. As in inside messages. Drums and guitars. Sounds crashing of car crashes. Singing. The way the sounds go louder louder the loudness you need.)

The parents go, make him explain.

I will not explain.

I can think hard thoughts. My IQ is such that.

I can think deep thoughts.

My mouth is glued shut.

(In comics there's more as in hidden pictures hidden words. The stories how they go on and on. Inside jokes we all know and so on.

In foods there's taste and the rest. And foods turn you strong. I need to be strongest. That is: of the school of the house.

After these is the rest. What you sometimes need: violence. What they think you need: school family females.)

We have made a circle.

The parents lean in. They go, explain.

I go, make me.

(All school is for the stupid meaning for the females. Birds should go to school and cows and dogs and rats. I know the most. The others have zero IQ. I have the highest of one hundred fifty. That is: more than my mother and brother combined. That is: more than the parents.)

The wall clock spins in slow speed. We have paper and pencils to make a deal.

(I have powers in the IQ and I am biggest.

My brother once knew a thing. Then once he was stupid. Then more so then more so. He has killed his whole head and I have seen it. I have caught it floating in a smoke cloud.

He is smaller.

The school is a place daytime and night. It's a place outside and in.)

Tonight is inside and quiet. In our circle the parents lean closer. They go, what are you writing?

I go, it's a free world.

(They should teach the birds and dogs a thing. They should make animals more like humans and females more like males and males more like superheroes.

I would go, poof! And the females disappear.

On my cap is lyrics and big deal. On my shirt is a comic and the females go, big freak! I go, takes one to know one!

I go, prove it!

Where I sit in school I can't see the females. On my cap is my number one lyrics worn backward. The others have to face it. Big deal, I go over my shoulder and, deal with it. They throw pencils. They make sounds like, sssssss. They go, fat!

Then down on my list. I pencil their names.

What you need isn't always what you want. For example when you need violence. They think we need school. And females.

And when my mother goes, is that a mustache, and comes closer. And when I run to my room and she follows. And when my brother slams his door and slams it and slams it.

And that my mother cooks and never eats. There are pies to cool. She watches us eating.

Foods will make me biggest. That is: a wall unbreakable.)

The parents have my list.

They go, take him from school. They go, bad bad, and such. Suspended! Troubled!

There are schools in the city. Special ones.

And it means: smaller buses. And it means: silent classrooms.

My mother goes, we'll talk.

She goes, what is it you want?

What is it? Well. I want and want and want. Nothing.

(Comics have big fights. I have seen the blood and the mess. I have seen a head on a sword. A heart on the ground.

The females shake in circles. Oh horrible bloody messes!

And I go, wet your pants little females. But superheroes conquer the negative, I go. They fix things.

Places. Worlds. Even if it means: violence. Even if it means: secret identities.

The females go, pervert.

But my brother is the one. He showed me the subliminal.

You have to read the lyrics. You have to listen forward and back. You have to play it low speed. There's words in words. Twistaround words that go all different ways. Then there's comics upside down. They plant messages inside. Skulls hidden in the clouds. Females in the ground. The lyrics tell you do this and then that. As in: violence. My brother goes I should listen. He goes, do what they say. He goes, you think you're smart, and smacks my head.

But I am getting bigger and bigger. An unstoppable wall.

I know certain backward lyrics. Mean things to say. That is: subliminally. And I will get big to shake them up. They go, freak. Fat fuck! I see them shaking.)

The parents go, we want to help.

I go, ha ha ha.

(My brother and I once had a club. We called it a name and had basement meetings. We made a birdcall for protection. And we had secret identities. We used the birdcall for trouble. No one gave us any. We were the two. I still remember how it goes like this:

[   ]

They go, too adult, and, grow up! My shirt and a shirt big deal. The females get shaken. It's only a comic. I could scream this. Stupid! They go, X-rated! and cover their faces. I put them on my list.

My shirt is the colors red and black. It has a picture and easy words made of letters. But look closely. Do they even see it?

They think too soft and never see it.

The females go, I'm telling! They fake cry in huddles but I've seen them at night. I've seen what they do when the school has shut. And there's my brother there slouched. The males all stand smoking. Females crouch and I have seen them there.)

The parents go, don't let him write. Take it. What is it?

And I go, it's a secret.

(My list has the teachers. The females. The others. Especially my brother. The bad comic writers. The lovesong writers. The wasters of time.

The females go, move it!

I pencil their names and they see me do it.

I think, poof! They disappear.

They go, we're telling, running. But they're scared. I am a hundred times their brains and size. I wear XXL. I am a wall unpassable.

Their IQ is a brain waste.)

The parents go, violent title.

They go, he is danger.

They go, why?

Why why why?

(The number one lyrics go, go fuck yourself! They go, you fucked up!

My shirt has harmless words. Just words scrambled and harmless that unscrambled say something different and harmful and you can get the message if you look close. Read it backward. Now read just every other word. Now the other every other.

Now look into the picture.

But prove it I go. Because normal first word to last means nothing bad. And words do nothing bad but scare. And pictures do nothing but scare. And once

you see the words and pictures they lose all power.
They're nothing.

In other words: you go between the lines to break
the power.)

The parents go, please then please.

No I can't is the problem. Ask my big IQ mother.

(My brother drives and with the females. And with
the males. They drive my mother's car. She has not
always said he can use it. They go to the school to
huddle behind. The lights have shut off. He forgets
the birdcall when I pass.

If dogs were more like humans I would take a dog.
I would throw my brother for him to chase and chew.
I would go, fetch! And he would bring my gnawed up
brother. And I would put us all in the basement. And
I would lock the door and make our club.

My mother used to put us in same color shirts.

They used to go, are they twins or something?

No, she would go. They're two years apart.

But I was already his size. Then bigger now biggest.)

The clock goes and goes.

I write this with this pencil. I write this now. Now
I write this with this pencil.

(My comics have females with big parts and wide
leg spreads in the subliminal. I can see them in the
background. My comics have superheroes and big
bloody fights and, big deal, I go. Some comics are
adult from adult words. They have the harmless fuck
bitch. They are held behind the counter. The guys go,
hiya big guy! Where's your brother been?

I have caught my brother's hair in his face. I have
caught his eyes rolled back. His pants pulled down.
Sweat on his brow. Panting.

I have caught females at his feet.)
The parents go, please explain the list please.
Ask my mother. She thinks she knows it all.
(When my mother cooks everything has to cool. I read at the table. She stares at us. My two, she goes. My brother gives me the eye without looking but I have powers in the birdcall:
[   ]
And again and again.
He forgets it. His hair drags. His skin is on a downhill. If I could go, poof! And he disappears.
My lyrics go, your parents don't know!
They go, do what you want!
My mother: shave the face hair.
I: give me a radio.
My mother: now!
I: with headphones.
A deal. And now I can't hear her.
Let the pies cool. My brother has no patience. He jabs through the crust. He is subhuman. I tell him. He calls me freak. He is android. His head floats in a smoke cloud. His skin is marked. His fist lands in the pies. On the tables. In my back.)
The parents call me troubled. The females are troubled. They stole my list.
Bad bad, go the parents.
They go, wait outside. I wait in the hallway.
(I listen through my headphones at the table. My brother mouths, fat freak! I turn the volume. His hair drags through the foods. He mouths, fat fat fat. My mother mouths, stop it all of you. She drinks water. The lyrics go, down down down down!
My mother goes, my little two.
She goes, you're staying home tonight!

My brother takes his jacket. He takes the car keys.
I can go through the backdoor unseen.)

Tonight the lockers look smaller. The classrooms
are locked. The windows are locked.

They could be out there now.

From the parents' circle in the room: come in! We
don't have all night.

From this place in the hallway: then turn the clock
fast speed!

(I see what happens at school at night. I have heard
them laughing. From behind the car I have seen the
smoke. I have seen what the females do crouched
like that. My brother's eyes are closed. The car radio
plays the lovesongs. My brother hates those love love
love. So he says so he said.)

The parents want a deal: a doctor.

And what would the doctor go?

Starve yourself fatty. Be nice fuck up. Grow up.

(My brother slams his door in the evening every
evening.

He never washes ever. He shoulders me and walks
out dirty.

Muffled through the headphones:

From the doorway: my little man is shaving!

From the kitchen: young man get in the car!

But the car was gone. We walked.)

And now. The parents: can you explain the list?

No explain how I have one hundred fifty and I
can't explain a thing.

(I have caught my brother against the school. I have
caught him moving. I have caught his hands in their
hair the car music playing.

I thought to take the car away. I thought to drive off
and far. The car could have been a rocket. A weapon.

I thought to shine the headlights on them. To crash into them. Bitches. Fuckers. I could have crashed them with the car.

Instead I walked past slowly. I gave the secret bird-call. I went, hiya! My brother straightened. He threw bottles. He went, fat fuck! The males went, freak! The females scrambled.)

The parents go, what did you mean?

(My brother could be out there now.)

Explain!

(The females could be out there too.)

Did I mean what I wrote? What did I mean writing? What could I have meant if not that? If not that that that then what what what?

The females' parents want to break me. They are zero IQ.

They go, are you violent?

They go, what are you writing?

My answers: no and nothing it's a free world.

And: read between the lines if you want my power.

They want me stupid. They want me little.

My mother cries. I have seen her shaking. I have heard her at my door but never crying.

I am one fifty IQ but my head is floating. Unglued. I am one twenty. One hundred. Eighty.

I go, the whole world is bad.

How is that then, and they lean in closer.

The whole world is bad. Can you see it?

I am forty thirty.

My mother goes, my little. Her hand comes close.

I am ten.

(If I had a dog I would throw my brother. I would go, fetch! And the dog would bring my bitten up brother. Caught! And I would hold my brother hostage in the basement. I would glue him to a wall. We would be the two. I would go in his face, females are stupid. School is for the stupid. Love is bad bad. Don't poke in the food. Don't throw bottles. I would make him clean. First his ugly marked face. Then his dragging strings of hair. There are three things worth anything. I would quiz him. What are the three things or poof!

And we would be the two.)

The parents lean in.

I go, the whole world. Don't you know this? This is where we're headed.

Where are we headed then?

I go, we're headed somewhere. I don't want to head there.

(I would give my brother the birdcall until he gave it back.)

The parents go, why?

The females go, sssssssss. Make them stop. You can't.

I am five and I only want these three. Comics. Foods. Music. Nothing else.

I will be as big as two.

They go, the list the list.

It's words, I go.

They go, please.

I go, it's nothing bad.

I throw my pencil. They lean in.

It's nothing.

Saturday

This is not about the hammer dug up from the yard.
I know you think something other.

But this is not about the good girl rooted at her
door. Nor her dwarf dog yelping. How it yapped underfoot and sprung. How it pawed our yard flying dirt
and roots and my mother dashed. She faltered. I froze
and fell. The dog chased its tail. Or was it trapped in
our chase? Well it ran in a circle as we too circled.

We had a warm spring day and the next day and
the next if I recall and the next before the truly hot
heat set.

But no one talks of the heat rising. No one talks of it growing hotter more hot. They talk of the chase. That I chased. My mother dashed. That I ran and froze and fell. I crumbled down into a pile. I held the hammer turned so the part that pulls nails faced out. An innocent error. I was no delinquent. I meant to hold it forward. I meant not to hold it.

I say the men did not have to turn so rough. To tug me this and that way. There was a time when I thought myself needful. I was giving forth goodness. Despite what you think and you think thoughts.

Try to turn them.

Think the sun shone. Think the grass felt less hot than inside. Think the house was bursting. One the lights. Two the radio. Three the oven. And on and on. It was a day for a run in the cool yard. Think the rusted swings how they swung out back. The weeds how they grew through yellowed newspapers. Through scattered envelopes. The sun shone vivid. Fruit flies shimmered in a swarm I ran through. They scattered and swarmed and I deserved a run in the yard.

A true story goes a man had to leave. My mother told him, get. Or that he left. There were continents for goodness sake. Who would avoid the globe with its continents of highlands and grasslands? Not he. He walked or crawled or took a bus a plane. Or he rode in a carriage. Or in a boat.

There was a brother and me both small and the man got and what do you think? You have thoughts. You think I am wrong. You think the man left from my wrongdoing. From my brother's. My mother's. You have thoughts enough but here.

Think the man was a magic man. A powerful man. A discoverer. Think of the invisible. Think of super. He had no choice you have to think.

Think then the man lived in one house and we in another. The man lived then in a farther away house. Then farther. Then his house was a speck and ours a speck but his since even binoculars could not help. Ours from size. His so even with a telescope pointed. We sat in the tree late nights pointing until I flat out could not.

This is not about my mother's head abloom with curlers. Nor her hair to be sprung loose. It would have curled and loosened by dinner. The man was close we knew by her curious mind-frame. Her joyful edge. He was coming for dinner and to us my mother said, shoo!

Under the bed is where I went. Under was the only place besides outside. Then I stood at the doorway to see the dwarf dog circle and dig. The good girl saw. It pawed up trash and toys. I went again to the under-neath. Then again to the doorway.

My mother cleaned. She polished. She wrung soaked rags. Her hair set tight rolled. Black lashes flipped. We knew of the dinner. There was no use her being hush hush. She stirred on the stove and inside the oven a cake rose. She swept and I knew under the bed was a mess of dust. I saw more dust than I ever saw. Dust formed good shapes of smoke and clouds. Though too much choked. When it coated the floor. When it clung too thick to the springs. Here clean under here, I told her. Bring your broom and make it clean. She went from room to room sweeping. She should have swept out under for the man to see my sleeping place. Come in here and sweep. She went from room to other room to other room.

He would travel in on a plane in a coach or cart. He would walk up arms spread or crossed or filled of gifts. I would come to greet him.

He would feel our house bursting. From the sidewalk he would. From the steps up through the doorway.

More than a decade we waited. I waited. The man lived somewhere in a house and lucky us we too had one. Lucky too with rooms enough just no good way out. We were in deep goodness stuck deep indoors. My brother said the man needed out. He had to see the globe which men do he said. Or worlds would never come forth he said. We would live in caves praising fire. Just think of those gloomy days. Goodness no. Someone had to make the fortune my brother said. Someone had to make the discoveries and why not the man he said. Yes why not and I would say to the man, tell me what is it you do. I would then say, welcome to this house. Do not mind the yard. He would rush up the steps rushing through the doorway. Come into the house you never saw. Certainly you wondered of it. Did you expect this hallway? This room or this? This place where I sleep? Come under.

He would bring spring flowers wrapped in paper and for goodness sake other treats. At last treats and to think she cooked him meat and cake. She ironed a dress. He would bring pets. What we deserved for being good. For keeping inside as my mother said to keep inside the house. Just inside. Not meaning the yard or out back. Keep away from the rusted swing set, she said. Do not go near the mailbox. There is no trouble inside so keep in for goodness. The only trouble comes from out. Meaning on the grass. Meaning in the gutter. My mother said to keep from the neighbors. Neighbors are the worst most troubled kind. And their rotten pets. Pets are the worst kind of dirty. Keep away from dogs. They carry fleas in their coats. Ticks and worms. And the street cats with their sharp rotted claws. They will claw you and spread their rot. And keep from the streets. Meaning the neighborhood ones and beyond. And not just on Saturdays but all days keep in. Go to school and come home straight. Not by way of the woods or the streets. Trouble comes from outside and we stayed in but from time to time my brother and I went out on the sly. From time to time we went to a place. The tree at the edge of the yard.

We went late. My mother slept sound. Still we crept. We dug in the dirt. We sat high in the tree. We looked up and around and below was the yard the street. There was hardly more than quiet. Leaves and insects flitting.

The good girl's house was shut down meaning no electric. Meaning quiet! for the day of Saturday. The good girl was a good Jew. Unlike me. Unlike my brother my mother. The girl was quiet with a scarf-covered head. And no carrying for her on a Saturday. None for the day meaning the poor dwarf dog could not be carried back into its house. It pawed the start of a tunnel in our yard. It chose our yard to any on the street. Ours bloomed. One yellowed newspapers. Two rusted toys. Three tall weeds. Four paw holes. And so on. No wonder the dog wanted to tunnel. I said, here's what we have for you. Meats and other foods. Come through the doorway here. Come look under where I go. Under is where I sleep. There is radio to hear there. I called, here! The girl did not even pet its fur. No wonder it chose me to her and her prayers and good. It chose our tattered yard over their proper grass square. Their fenced-in squares of flowers.

You think that I am wrong but here. The dog came. I dangled no meat even. I held out an empty hand and here it stepped a dwarf paw over the threshold. Two paws. Closer. Three.

Do you think that I am mean? You have these thoughts of me since the good girl could not yell as her dog stepped four dwarf paws inside. She could not come and clutch it. She froze face against the screen. Her father close behind. I am not unfair. The dog chose. I could not rush out either so watch your thoughts.

The man left some things useful on any continent. A shirt. A hammer. A telescope. I thought to wear his shirt. To walk the globe until he noticed his stains. His holes. He would leap from a chair from a car from a step and stop me. Or I would tap his hammer on the sidewalk. I would knock it on the streets. If he heard his hammer clang he would follow and there! His hammer. His own stained shirt. His good one. But the hammer was rusted old. The shirt a worthless rag.

My mother said, keep from his things. He'll want them.

We wrapped the telescope and hammer in the shirt and buried them deep in a hole by the tree. We used the telescope for night looking. The hammer for in case of trouble.

You know I wanted the girl to step one foot forward. I wanted to see her scowling face dragged back in by her scarf.
You know the dog came to me on its own.
I am not mean. The dog stepped back out.

In the tree we sat high. We swatted insects and I went out farther. Then farther to the farthest point out and I fell.
I looked up to my brother my mother. They hovered. The grass was wet. I asked for the hammer I know. Safe hidden. The telescope. Safe below. I got carried in to the insides.

I would show the man under the bed. The way to go under. How to lie on the floor. To flatten out. To slide slowly under until there is darkness. Then light comes from a flashlight. Then look up and around. See how shapes grow into places? How springs are buildings? How dust is tumbleweeds and dogs? See the cows the cars the tornadoes the cornstalks the skyline? The sound comes from the radio. Let's sing to it. I know the words.

This is not about my mother stepping out for the mail. This is not about how I swung open the door. My mother needed to get in. She stood in the gutter in curlers. In her robe. She opened envelopes littering the yard the girl watching. The dog barking. I knew to pull her in before the whole globe knew ours. The dog snapped as if to give a bite.

One car drove past. Two. And someone called, shameful, from either the girl's house or from a car. Someone thought her shameful. Well yes all undone in the gutter. Head rolled up in colors.

I said, get in!

She would have to get or the man would see. I could see plainly. The neighbors could. She would send him again by standing waiting. She did once send him by saying to get. Or he wanted out. To think he could arrive from an old decade and see her blooming head. The dwarf dog hanging teeth sunk into her bare leg. He would run again.

She needed first to get in. Second to unroll her hair. Third to dress and hurry with dinner. It would burn.

I knew to round her up before the dog roused the street. It yelped a frightful yap. Everyone glanced through windows to see my mother standing head rolled bright. Robe nearly opened. The dog snapping at her bare ankles. Envelopes dropped on the weedy grass. I said, get in! The girl pressed at her screen. She would have pressed herself straight through but she could not press harder. Her father's eyes were on her. His Saturday eyes. One foot forward and she would have been in trouble. She knew too. She watched herself. She prayed I know. If only she stepped out though. I wanted the fireworks and her dog. I deserved her dog for being good. I should have stepped out to say, we're having a dinner! A dinner with the four! One me. Two my brother. Three the father. Four my mother. And none of you!

But no one cared about the cake in the oven.

No one talks that I slept on the floor. To help my spine. Not to hurt it. Do you understand this? That I suffered when I fell from the tree? That I slept on the floor to fix my spine? And not just on the floor but under in the springs' world. For coolness. Do you understand? That I often crumbled down into a pile? When just walking eating. Down! I crumbled. Down in a loose hill of bones. Anyone could have scattered my pieces. Bits of me by the mailbox. Parts in the gutter. There in a paw hole. But I do not need to talk of suffering. We had a very good time climbing the tree. I moved out farther on the farthest high branch. My brother said nothing and the branch snapped clean. I shook out from the tree and worse. My spine. But this is not about my brother pulling me up from the dirt. How he knocked my head later and said, is anyone home? How I wanted the hammer. The telescope. Hidden in time. I wanted isolation. I preferred the place under. A place of meadows and bluffs and quiet. Thank goodness for those worlds. The ones unmapped. Double spider webs in corners. Dirt trapped in floor cracks.

What I remember before he got. He was a man. He owned a tattered shirt a telescope a rusted hammer. He left them. He took a train a bus a jet a boat but we were too small and I smaller. Smallest so I remember nothing. My brother remembers he was a scientist mathematician. A bus driver astronaut. He made discoveries of sorts. We cannot live without discoverers.

No one wants to cave dwell. I know what I was told. To think invisible. Super. Man in the moon. Look up for him with the telescope. Hold it close to your eye like this. Then squeeze the other one shut tight like this. Then turn the middle. Or was it the bottom? Look up and focus. Think of a face. The one you want. Sometimes he shows. Sometimes you have to wait.

My brother dug up the telescope for window look-ing. Even for the insides of the good girl's house. I saw him from below late nights looking.

At the dwarf dog, he whispered. It did tricks at night. It raised its paws to shake hands. It rolled. It stood and danced a dance step.

I could not climb the tree with my brittle spine. I wanted to see.

He whispered, it jumps through hoops. It wears a scarf.

He said, get.

I told my brother to bring her in. Goodness I was cross-eyed with it. It was his mother too for goodness sake in the gutter. I said, the man is on his way.

My brother said flat out, wrong man.

He said, this is another man. A new man, he said. A man for a dinner date. An outside date. A different man. They had met, he said. They were going into the outside for a dinner.

But who is what I needed to know.

He said, to a place with food. To a special dark place. Where you cannot go and I cannot.

I asked where though.

He said to forget the man. There was never the man. Go away.

The meat and cake was ours then.

My brother watched from his window. He watched his shameful joyful mother in the gutter undone. He watched like another troubled neighbor as the dog yelped up her bare leg.

The girl stood face pressed to her screen and what a good girl wearing that bright scarf her face pressed tight. I bet her screen smelled like a thunderstorm. Ours did. I swung out the door and screamed, a storm!

What a scowl she could put forth. What a good one keeping wrapped up inside.

Come on out, I called to the girl. Come and get your dwarf dog.

It yelped good and hard. My mother took no notice.

I would have said, I'll do this for you, to the man. For you since we need you here. You in our bursting house and not some other outsider. Not some other taking her into the outside for a dinner. For you and I will round her up before the world knows ours.

But this is not about my charge-taking.

This is not about troubled neighbors stepping onto trimmed yards.

I should have said, the show is over! I should have said, step back over your thresholds! Look away! I should have.

This is not about keeping indoors stuck inside and I stepped forth one foot. I stepped forth two. I said, shameful! I said it clear from outside.

I said, get inside!

She stood reading robe opening. The dog circled her ankles yelping. Neighbors stepped closer. I stepped to the tree. To the dirt pile filling the hole.

She said, get inside!

My brother looked. Scared he looked and I dug in the dirt pile for the rusted hammer.

My brother never did admit that yes I talked as the one who took charge. He never did admit I won square. I charged her back inside. You think it was selfish. You think I thought of me alone. But my brother ate all the meat the next day. He got all the cake. The man had a clean good one to come to. My clean mother locked up covered in her safe room the whole next week. Who got thanks? Well certainly not me. Who got hurt? Who do you think?

I knew her hair would have sprung curls and sure blame me. Her ironed spring dress would have looked lovely. No blame for my brother his head stuck through the window then not. No blame for the man long gone on a continent. He was needed elsewhere for discoveries. No blame for the very good girl. Had I not helped though what do you think? My poor mother.

What would you have done? Are you aware of a plan two? Would you have reversed your mind-frame? Would you have kept good in the springs' world? Would you have sweet-talked by the gutter? Sweet-talked up the stairs? Helped her in? Helped out? I was crossed with these and other routes. But the sun shone clear through her robe.

This is not about cars parked slanted. Everyone stood crammed into their yards. I was no delinquent. A quick haze grew rushing up in a swarm. I was tugged this way that way. They cuffed only one wrist. Was this supposed to scare me? All I was doing was yelling. The other cuff swung forth. They took away the hammer. I was not going to use that. My brother closed his window. Through the haze I saw him go.

This is not about the back seat and boy it was hot. They caged me. I swung the loose cuff to break through the cage. I swung to break the window for air. I pounded and called and the haze circled my mother. The haze of arms and other trouble. I say they did not have to crowd her so. She stood troubled shameful in curlers and spilling from her robe and the dwarf dog tried to climb her. She hated dogs. It followed her across the yard. The whole haze followed her from place to place. The hammer sat there on the dirt.

The girl watched mouth gaping but this is not about her nor how her yard looked better than ours with the right round shrubs and the swept walk. This is not about how she opened her door for a better look nor how she stepped one fancy-shoed foot forward and her father dragged her from her doorway slamming shut the door and I said, I saw you carry! I said it through the sealed windows. Through the spinning blue I said, I saw you bad Jew!

The dog kept by my mother's feet.

The car door opened.

My poor mother.

They did not lock the car door so who was to blame?

I would have said, let me fix you a plate. Sit. Tell me about the globe. What is the coast about? Tell me about the desert. Have you seen live sheep? Live horses and other cattle? I will hang your coat. Would you like your shirt ironed? It has a small stain. Would you like it washed? Now tell me about your house. Does it have trees surrounding? Does it have swings? Windows? Lawn chairs? A trim of shrubs? Is there a swimming pond? Do you have anyone else? A cook? A maid? Please here is a drink. Would you like more ice? Here is a plate. A fork. Put up your feet. What lovely looking shoes. Were they costly? Take a rest. Tell me about the decade. What did you think about? What did you do? Have you ever seen a live volcano? A live tornado? An earthquake? A monsoon?

Are you a mathematician? I thought not. A scientist? No I thought not.

Please come under. Look what I can see. Can you see it too? That I am a discoverer? That I have traveled the globe? Can you see how worlds start from springs? From hair and lint? From dust?

My mother kicked the dog with a bare foot. My soon to be pet. The men laughed. She too. My brother too from the doorway. And the neighbors. The haze of mouths gaping laughing. The mailbox laughing. The gutter and the good girl too and her bad father held his side I know inside their house and the whole street went on and on as I fled the car. No one saw as I pulled the hammer from the dirt. I clutched it tight and I was no delinquent. I will never say it despite the street's word. I was no wrong-doer. Goodness what a fallen lawn. The newspapers piled. The envelopes

sprouted there and there. A haze of weeds and holes.
Men's arms and mouths and horrible fruit flies. Who
did not know of a man coming? Which one person in
which trimmed yard did not know of an outside date?
I screamed this yes I cried and my mother laughed.
The men held her tight steady. Raise a hand if you do
not know. Sure it was a dinner date and she was soon
to be dolled up. Everyone knew. Look at her spilling
from her robe. Blooming like a spring garden. Everyone knew. She laughed a joyful laugh and everyone
saw. She had no business on this day growing through
the sun haze. Through my cross-eyed rage. Through
the fruit fly swarm. She was blooming bridging growing clear up and over falling toward the ground. Flower
stalks burst from her head and they bent and swayed
and she drooped about to hit the grass. The flowers
grew wild and lucky I had the hammer to tap. She
was erupting and I needed to help her. I needed to
stop her. And who did not know? Her hair soon to be
curled. The haze around her tightening. Arms around
her tighter. The neighbors eyed our clutter. My brother
eyed but did not try to stop me. He never tried to stop
me. When I went farther to the farthest point I fell.
The branch snapped clean. I cried and waked my
mother. I waked the neighbors. My mother swung open
the door. She stood above me. I should have stayed
put. I should have stayed inside.

The curlers would have cracked under the hammer
sure but anything was better than her blooming. And I
had the hammer held backward by error. I never meant
to swing. The dog yapped underfoot. I circled my
mother. She turned in a circle. We ran. I went to swing.

I said, shoo!

This is not about how my spine caved in and I crumbled into the yard holes mid-swing.

This is not about my mother crumbling. How her hair never sprung. It unrolled flat. She burst and sunk crying on the curb over what? I never could decide.

I do not think I meant to hurt. I was trying to guide. To help. Both the dog and my mother. The neighbors. My brother. The man. Do you understand this? That I was pouring forth goodness and everything was a haze around and above me?

This is not about the car radio static and the street hissing past. I was a hill on the hot back seat. And was it my brother who made the call? Was it he who let them pluck me from the weeds? He who let them lock me up? They quizzed me and shouted and I spent the night on a thin cot with a bent spine in a locked room but I found the place under the cot with its narrow springs. I saw its dust and cracked floor and dried insects of a meadow and the sun came in.

Everyone knew the man never showed. Which man though? Well no man.

Good thing. We did not need trouble again from the outside.

I had summertime in the underneath. I let the dwarf dog in on Saturdays. We had a time me petting his fur talking in our isolated underneath. I had the voices for the tumbleweeds. For the cows and clouds. Upside down and under the springs made a farm. The bed legs made soaring skyscrapers. A sheep-filled meadow. This until the bed collapsed. And this from my brother jumping hard with me and the dog under and lucky no one got hurt.

This is not about how I dragged home the next warm morning with my brother. This is not about how the good girl swung the hammer for a laugh as I rounded the corner and my brother did nothing. This is not about how the hammer had been in the yard forever. How it got brought up again and again. Not the hammer but the story. They talk of the chase. Of sirens of blue lights of the street damaged dragged down. A kicked dog. An open robe. A body crumbled. Mine it was. And my screaming poor mother in the chase and I. I gripping a rusted hammer one hand cuffed. Would it change the story to say I was a delinquent? To say I was not trying to help? To say how the man never showed? Or how my brother crushed the telescope? How he threw away the tattered shirt? How the girl kept the hammer in her house? How I never learned the man's name? Moonman. Super. Nowhere. How I went back to school on Monday?

testing,

because you never listen, because you sit there not
listening on your cloud, are your ears on, testing testing, because there are bullies, because you ask to be
bullied, because you ask for trouble, because I taught
you how to punch, because it's tricky out there, it's
merciless, and you never punch, because you sit there
not punching and fists are flying, because I'm on to
your fear, because you need to be fearless, can you
hear me, testing, because you need to live large, you
need custom made, because a custom car is everything, because customized makes you a star and I feel
like a damn star in here, because that's all, I'm finished, do you ever feel like a star, because you're still

young, there's time left, because there are worse places:
the hospital, the street, should I turn around, should I
drive you back, because there are places worse than
this custom car, you could have it far worse, I swear,
you could live on the street with that way you look,
that hair, that coat, you could be in the hospital hooked
to tubes, don't get me started, because I'm finished
talking now, I'm driving now, because this is for your
own damn good, because you get F's and F's are for
failure failure, repeat after me, and your brother gets
B's, your brother's been trashed, because it's merciless out there, they trashed him good, but there's a
way to shine, I swear, to use your brain, because you're
acting dull and I'm on to your act, because you need
to live larger, because you're part of the tribe, the same
damn blood, because we wandered the desert with
fire and so forth, because we're put to the test, because who doesn't punch when fists are flying, because this is your time, you're young, do you want to
shine like your brother or do you want dullness, because I told you so, I warned you, didn't I warn you,
I tried to tell you, but you never listen, because your
music is loud and I hear your music, you think I can't
but I know music, it makes you dull and you're not
dull, I swear, because even you could drive a custom
car: six cylinder, two-toned and so forth, I swear, because even you could have it all: automatic, power,
plush interior, but first you have to work some, because you'll always be tested, repeat after me, because
you could end up like that one, you could end up like
that one, or you could be a star, I swear, you could
marry a doctor, a star like your brother, he wants to be
a doctor, I've said it all, I'm driving now, because you're
not dull, really, you could shine, you're just troubled,

because I smell the smoke coming from your room, you think I don't, but I see the smoke and I know it's trouble, don't get me started, because I care, the neighbors care, because the bullies watch you, I see how they watch you how they stare and I hear how they talk, because you have holes in your coat and who walks around in holes and you have dirt on your coat, because your hair is snarled, a tangled nest, because what good doctor wants a girl with snarled hair, because it's time to use your brain and I know you have a brain under that nest, you look dirty but I know you're clean, you need to start caring, because time is passing, you won't be young always, because a week of punishment is a good thing, because a week of sitting and thinking can only be good, because your music dulls you, I'm taking your music, because you need to have quiet, a week to think, because you've turned hateful, troubled, why are you so hateful, you never say hello and your brother loves you, I swear, he wants to help you, because you could end up like that one or that one, living on the street, because I know you're good and I know you're clean, but that color is fake and it looks like a nest and everyone talks, the bullies, I hear them and your brother hears them, because he knows how to listen and you never listen, testing testing, come in from your cloud, because your brother had a scrap and if your brother can have a scrap with all he's got going: straight B's and so forth, mercy, well then, what about you, snarled hair, straight F's, mercy, and you look like a girl who gets F's, I swear, don't get me started, because you could have a scrap, because you ask for trouble, because what good doctor wants a dull girl, because your coat is torn, you have a new coat, wear it, because you

have a nice true color, brown, like mine, what's wrong
with brown and brush it, because bullies will drag
you down, because they will take you wrong and treat
you wrong, they will use you and wrong you, I swear,
they will see a troubled face under that nest and they
will use you up and mess you up, mercy, don't start
me, they will say things, I swear, don't you want to
shine, because your brother shines, because he can
take a punch, because he can take a fist to the eye
and he knows to be fearless you have to punch back,
you have to be fearless, testing testing, because you're
part of the tribe, you're a Steinberg and I taught you
how to punch, because I won't always be here, do
you remember how to punch, because I taught you
how to live, because you're a girl and it's harder for
girls, your brother won't always be here, so show me
your punch, because a fist to the face can break a
face, a fist to the head can rattle a skull, repeat after
me, and you have to extend, follow through, you have
to be tricky, there's a girl way and a man way, be a
man when you punch, be a girl when you walk, when
you speak, when you dress, when you sit, because
sometimes it helps to be girl-like, hair brushed, sugar
in this shit world, because we all need some sugar, a
roof for example, repeat after me, because we suffered, we wandered the desert for years for what, for
this: for cars, for B's, for roofs above, because we didn't
wander the desert for F's, we didn't wander to hide
our blood, because the brown hair you have under
that nest, you got that from me, because you're my
blood, and some day you'll come down from your
cloud, you'll look at yourself, you'll see your true color
is nice and brown, it'll always grow out nice and brown
and you'll always look like a part of the tribe, because

I can see it clear, because you're not getting younger, because soon you'll leave the nest and where will you go, because there's a way to make a life and there's a way to go nowhere, your brother's going somewhere, because he took a shiner, because they called you names, because he heard the names and you didn't hear them, because of your music, your cloud, because you have it all: a room, a roof, you live large, you do, and I saw how the doctors watched you, because they watched me like I wronged you, tell me, is there a roof over your head or is there a roof over your head, tell them tomorrow, there's a roof, or we could tell them now, should I throw it in reverse, should we go back and tell them, you could tell them I help, I care, the neighbors care, because you're soft and your brother's hard, a stone, a skull like a stone, he'll pull through with a skull that hard, because I'm telling you so, because you're my blood, you're a Steinberg and Steinberg means mountain of stone, so act like a damn mountain of stone, because someday you'll be by yourself, because what doctor loves a fearful girl, because when you need to punch you need to be fearless and you need to remember to give some sugar, not just shit, because we all need some sugar, this car for example, this car's got punch: speed, power, sixty in seconds and look how they stare, look how they talk, because sometimes you need to get there fast, because sometimes there's a call when you don't expect a call, because sometimes you need to leave your work, you need to speed through streets, because the neighbors call when they call, mercy, at least the neighbors called, because sometimes time is ticking quick, because sometimes you need a doctor and fast, because I've said enough, because starting now you're

punished, one week, starting when we get home, because you have to think, because you were given a
life and this is your time, because that's life and life is
what, tell me, what is life, can you tell me, what is life
when your brother took it hard, when his skull rattled
good, what is life when we're just bones and blood,
because a skull is softer than stone, your brother's just
blood and scrapes, hooked to tubes, softer than stone,
so what is life, because your brother took a shiner and
you sat in your room, because his poor head rattled
and you sat in your room, because he fell to the ground
and you sat in your room, hiding because there was
blood on the walk, on the grass, on the house, my
blood, your blood, because you sat there not listening, fists were flying, you sat there not looking, your
music turned loud, in a cloud of smoke, because what
were you thinking when they called you names, what
were you thinking when your brother threw a punch,
when the bullies punched back, what were you thinking when they called you trash, the neighbors said so,
trash, they said the bullies said when they called me
sounding fearful, trash, they said, because brown hair
makes you nice and this color makes you fake and
your brother deserves better, a nicer sister, a car when
he's stronger: eight cylinder, two-toned, custom and
so forth, because he's ready to feel like a star, because
he's been through the shit: ultra plush, FM, three-toned,
because he's holding tight while you fall apart, because he could open his eyes any time, he could say
hello, because we're the chosen tribe and you need
to be nice, you need to look nice and tomorrow tell
your brother hello because he loves you, I swear, he
wants to help, because you could be a star or you
could be like that one, roofless, lifeless, trash, only

worse, because you're just a girl, because you're no longer young, because time is ticking, no matter how hard you punch me, harder, stronger, punch like a man, because your time is ticking and you punch like a girl and you look like trash and I taught you better, you look like trash and you need to extend, you need to follow through, you need to punch me harder, harder, punch like a man and follow with sugar, because tomorrow your brother could open his eyes, he could say hello, and you could be there shining in your new coat and brushed brown hair when he does because he could keep his eyes closed after that and deep down you're not trash, you're not trash, you're not trash, repeat after me, you are a mountain of stone

Away!

The way to steal a car is to first become invisible and the way to become invisible is to have good concentration. It is about seeing under your skin with your inside eyes. When everything gets glittery you will slowly fade.

You have to fade into nothing to steal the car. The reasons are obvious. The plan is as follows.

Concentrate. Steal a car. Drive the car to New York City. Leave the car in a dark lot. Stay in New York City so you can become famous. Do not get caught doing anything corrupt or your mother will come to get you. She will touch your face when you are riding home on the bus and her hand will feel strange and cold

like you are her long lost love and there is no worse
feeling.

Invisibility is to be taken seriously. Chances are no
one will believe what you can do. Remember it is a
necessary part of self-improvement. You will need to
become invisible to steal the car. You will need the
car to get to New York City. New York City will make
you famous. Then you will certainly be improved.

To prepare for invisibility your walls and windows
need to be painted black with glow-in-the-dark stars
stuck on so it looks just like outer space. Stand against
your walls like another star. You have to concentrate
and become a part. At some point you will want to
peel off the stars with a knife for important reasons.
Reasons to do with self-improvement.

In the dark time before you walk to the bus stop
you will see everything more clearly. Love and hate
will swim across the room at you in wavy pictures.
Use this time to plan. Think about how to get fame
and money. When you steal the car you will be feeling more free. You will go as fast as you can to New
York City.

(The color of the car is irrelevant but dark is obvi-
ously better so try the black one.)

Do not forget there are times when you will be quite
vivid. When there are loud noises. Mirrors. Crying. In

your bed at night before you are sleeping you will be only almost invisible like an x-ray or a jellyfish. Something translucent but still solid and there and you will shimmer. You will float in and out.

You will almost always be visible to yourself even when you are invisible to others. You will be able to see yourself in the mirror but it will often be a semi-transparent version of you because sometimes your face will be a thin clear layer and you will see the wall behind you. You will know you are there filling a space in the room the way you know where all your parts are in the dark.

Stare down the girls at the bus stop and think, you could not see me now if you wanted. Well I can tell you how I look. Very small very big very dark very bright.

When you claim to be invisible your mother will take you downtown to a tall building to see the doctors. They will tempt you with soft voices. Do not cry or you will be super vivid. The doctors will ask you questions about things you could have done corrupt. Stare out the window and let your mother look at her fingernails. She will answer the wrong way all the questions.

The doctors will sound like they are talking into microphones when they talk down to you. They will say, do you have friends? They will say, do you feel lonely?

Your mother will fear the doctors. They will write things down in black notebooks. So will you. Do not tell them you are planning to steal a car. Do not tell them you stole other things.

Your mother will cover her face because you will insist that you are invisible. The doctors will insist that you are troubled. Do not let their words threaten you. Your mother will be carrying on. But you will be magic. And how is that for a vast improvement?

The important thing is that we are all here in this world now just being here and the rest. We have all survived this place. We are spinning together and no one can stop us. We are spinning together at such a speed that we are stuck to the ground. At the same time that we are spinning we are shooting uncontrollably into the stars. Something is going to make us snap back into ourselves someday and then everything we once touched will blow apart.

Try to steal some girl's love away. He would feel so good with your invisible hands touching all over his skin. Better than how he feels now when he has to look at her. When you steal him away the girl will hate you for reasons of jealousy. But you will hate her for even bigger ones. She always talked down to you.

You will learn all about how boys can be soft. They will still be hard but with you they will be hard and soft.

(Concentrate into the glittery world. Away! You are invisible. Slip into the car unnoticed.)

You have to be very careful because sometimes an alarm in a store when you steal will make you reappear and then you will be caught with things from the store in your coat pockets. You will always remain visible until your mother comes to pick you up. It is embarrassing to get caught stealing because you are not a thief. Your mother will look worn out when she comes to get you at night. Her lipstick will be smeared from putting it on on the bus. At the police station you will always be very vivid in an orange chair. Not just visible but shockingly so. You will think, look at what I did corrupt. I'll never be anyone. But this is just practice for stealing the car which is the second step to true fame.

Your mother will wait for you at the bus stop under a broken umbrella. Make yourself invisible before you get on the bus to the doctors. On the way you will think that is some mascara your mother wears. Say, you act like being invisible is a problem. Imagine your mother is nowhere.

Around the doctors you have to stay calm. Their glasses will be all wrong. They will try to tap into your head but your head will be floating.

Just keep your mind set on the car. You have to think you are racing up the highway. You are changing the stations and the windows are open.

You will crush New York City under your new stolen shoes by stepping down hard. It will try to drag you around by your hair but you will crush it under your new stolen shoes by stepping down hard hard until you can feel the sidewalk cracking. In the wet streets you will see the sky and trees and buildings and you will step down hard making them splinter and wave away and you will look down at all of this in a way you never could before. You will find fame if you follow the steps.

The doctors will ask you about your dreams. Your dreams will be vivid. Do not tell them everything. In your bed each night you will be flat on your back. Your skin will crawl and rest and crawl again. Then everything will depend on what you are dreaming and you will ordinarily dream of one of two things: outer space or water. When you dream of water sometimes you will be in the ocean and the girls from the bus stop will be floating behind you and you will not be able to turn around to see them because you will be wearing heavy equipment or because there will be seaweed twining your neck.

Try to steal some girl's love away. It is good practice that will give you that feeling in the hot negative space around your head.

In your black room with the lamp on as dim as it will go plan things for your new life in New York City. Keep two knives flat under your mattress. A big sharp one for peeling off the stars. A thin pointy one for stealing the car. Both can protect you in case things turn bad. Expect to be hated for the wrong reasons. The important thing is that you are on your way. And no one will be able to see you.

(Jam the knife into the ignition. You know how to do this.)

Imagine the girls are dancing together at the bus stop with their big radio playing on the sidewalk. Their round knees stick out in their tights. You want to dance with them. They laugh at you. Concentrate. You see the underside of your skin fading. Everything is getting glittery. You are semi-transparent and now invisible and you can dance behind the girls and with them. Dance right up in their faces. You are a good dancer. They cannot see you laughing at them.

Above your heads the trees wave their thin branches and the spring snow is falling circling your heads and the sky is getting lighter. The bus whistles down the street and you float up on it together with the radio still playing but softly now. You are going to school the place that is nothing but you have a secret and you were really dancing.

There are words the big ones the doctors will use. Your mother will whisper them into her fists. When the words come up stare out the window of the office. Stare into traffic and let the cars run over your eyes. The doctors will talk. You will sigh and cough. Your mother's face will shatter. Try to understand the true meaning of the big words and how they taste metallic. You are not troubled. You are not lonely. You will make yourself laugh. You will laugh until your sides hurt.

(The car starts with a shake.)

Everyone has always wanted to be locked in a grocery store when it closes at night. This is everyone's biggest dream to be locked in a grocery store. Do this for practice. Eat whatever you want. Sit in the corner of the bakery eating a cake. Expect that the guard will find you. Expect him to point a gun at you and yell. Expect to become super-visible. The guard will call the police. The police will call your mother. Your mother will be mad at you because you do have food in the house. You always have plenty of food even a cake from the same grocery store. This is only practice.

Imagine kicking giant holes in New York City. Taking the fastest elevators to the tops of tall hotels. Riding the trains with your face pressed to the windows. The city will try to lose you in a rush of importance but you will be right there emerging from a manhole on a quiet tree-lined street.

School is the place that is nothing. You float through the halls as if you are nothing. It is the place where the winter sun shines through the windows and cuts you into dusty pieces. Your skeleton flashes in your hands. You are visible because school is loud.

You are never the star of anything.

Brush past in the halls like a sexy cat. Make your skin purr. Rub against lockers. You have long pretty claws for tearing out eyes that look at you wrong. No one deserves to look at you. To touch your hair. Remember. When you are famous none of this will matter. Keep your eyes clear and cold when the sun pours in from the windows. Concentrate. Even though it is loud. Even though your hands are flashing.

Stand up against your walls and belong there. Float there like a star.

Remember. Do not cry because it feels better to be in the shadows anyway and there is nothing worth crying about.

(Just slide out of the parking space as though the car is yours.)

Take a ride downtown on the bus with strangers moving at the same fast speed together. You need to prowl for the car to steal. The bus driver will look at you through his mirror until you disappear. Let him hurl you out there at the speed of light with his red eyes glued to the rearview. Let him hurl you and the others through the city like you are on a rocket traveling at the speed of light. There will always be that orange-gray sky. The rain will always whip the moving windows.

You will dream of space. You will fly in a silver suit with a big round helmet. You will know that if the helmet were to fall off you would breathe in tar. Whole galaxies will spin around themselves and black holes will try to suck you in. You will hold the helmet tight at your neck while comets sail past your head. You will learn the secret to flying in loops so they will not hit you. If you were to turn around you would see your house floating behind you like a moon.

You have always been many different people. The one to you and the one to the girls. The one to your mother. The one in your dreams. But soon you will be just one person.

You will notice the car you want one night when you are prowling and invisible. Trust me. You will find the one with the unlocked doors and the easy ignition.

They will only find you because of a mistake. So be careful because like almost everyone you are not perfect. Remember. You slam your fingers shut in your locker door to feel something hot.

You never drink at parties. You never dance with a group of crowding boys. There are never eyes and hands all over you. You never feel beautiful. And to think. Soon.

(You are really moving.)

You never know how it is to have someone's hands in your back pockets in the halls at school.

When you steal someone's love you will feel a temporary current in the space between both your heads. Something like a charge.

There will be something like a charge and your head will feel full of ice. Your insides will try to fly away. From down on the bathroom floor the lines of clouds out the window will look like a ribcage. Planes will float through the sky as boats swimming sailing sinking away into the lines of clouds. The bathroom floor will swallow you.

There will be something like a charge and then he will disappear and you will disappear.

Your mother will say, she's having a hard time. The doctors will say, would you care to talk? They will try to trick answers out of you. Have a good laugh at their serious faces.

(This is about becoming invisible and famous but first it is about staying awake all night.)

You will climb over cars and buses and trains and stores. Trust me. You will tear bricks out of buildings. You will steal money and slash tires and paint your name on walls and under bridges. New York City will try to murder you. It will offer you ways to disappear but by then you will already know how.

The doctors will say, but we can see you.
You will look at your mother. She will look out the window into traffic.
Do not let them break you down.

You never walk to the bus stop with girls practically running it is so freezing cold out with every step step step your ankles made of solid ice and the words shaking loose from your mouths until you are all laughing so hard at nothing.

You will be invisible at the doctor's office with your mother. One two three four and you will be gone. They will all be jealous. You will be asked to speak and your notebook will be floating in the air. They will think you are incredibly powerful. You will know then that you are good enough to steal the car.

In bed you will swim deep under water and there will be flowers growing and slowly swaying when you move past and millions of rows of little houses made of rocks and shells with tiny windows.

Remember. You are not the one who is troubled. The doctors will prescribe pills for you even though you feel fine. They will use words to make you less than them.

They will loan you books that you will not read. Take the pills if you want. They will make your dreams more vivid.

Ask the doctors, what about the big bang though? We are suffering from that. We are all spinning at the same speed being hurled out into space waiting to snap back into ourselves.

Say to a stranger on the bus, you will snap back too you know. To the girls at the bus stop to the doctors to your mother. Say, you cannot see me but right now I am looking okay.

Love and hate will fly through your bedroom.

When you are ready peel the stars off your walls with the knife. You will not need them anymore.

When your mother comes into your room without knocking pretend to be asleep. She will say, what happened to the stars? You will feel translucent. Your insides will be flying away. Your mother will quietly touch your back and keep her hand there until you start to feel tired. Concentrate.

(You like the way the seat feels. It is soft. The radio. Turn it on. Roll down the windows. Take the car out to the highway. Look. No other cars are in sight. You are really moving. Forget about your mother. Her hand is not really there you have to think.)

If you are not careful you will make a tremendous mistake. If you are not careful you will fall asleep and dream of outer space. You will fly in loops and feel very free but hours later you will wake up in your bed. And then what?

The End of Free Love

Locking is our word we made in May.

These others don't know from words or locking.
They fake zombie-walk. They call it locking when
they're fakers walking a zombie way.

As in faking blindness arms stuck out how we did
in our rooms as kids. As in Helen Keller how we
knocked into walls, I'm blind I'm blind.

As in drinking sips of syrup. The okayed dosage.
Then, look at me here! I'm locking hard!

As in drinking nothing but frenching a drinker and
they call it a contact lock.

And they widen their eyes like in the sixties saying,
wow man, and, far out I'm seeing spectral.

Though it's not called locking if you don't lock up. As in stiffened limbs. As in narcosis. Rigor mortis.

Not meaning dead but close.

A critical dose will fly your soul to outer lands. Meaning foreign lands with foreign words and triple moons.

The most critical dose turns to crystal lands then to waterfalls. Meaning a void potential meaning closest to dead.

But you don't want the void.

You want the syrup as fire-water. But it's made all of fire that blankets your soul.

And calling it fire is our invention. These fakers call it red sauce and they say they're sauced. Proof they don't know from words. Even though all their talk talk talk. We call them The Invasion all their talking. Their chirp chirp chirp. It's proof they're not locking.

Only faking and crashing make you talk. Meaning clear and in out loud words.

Besides. Look at their eyes. How to prove someone's locking is by the eyes. If there's a spark they're faking. If there's life they're fake.

But if there's overall vacant we say they're locking. Meaning Night of the Zombies with flat black eyes.

And we get ours flattest. Voided. Ask any.

We truly lock with triple vision. Size mutation. Telepathy and inner gravity loss.

We know who's fake. Their bright-lit eyes.

They're Land of the Lost we say telepathic but they can't hear us. They're all loose-limbed and static-souled.

These fakers live on the high-up streets of all the streets. In a high-up high-rise. And high-ups will turn all high-rise they say and bulldozers and wrecking balls. Meaning cabins wrecked and flattened.

All for hard cash and rib restaurants.

We say who needs high-ups when lowers have the boardwalk and arcades with songs? Our lower has cabins and cabins have beds and windows and ocean vistas past the windows.

We invented the soulful lower life.

These fakers come to our lower at night. They came last night. Faculties ordered. The last night of their summer. Then back to school. Good riddance we thought. Go back.

We were ready for the ocean alone. Just us two through fall. Through winter and onward. And neither mother. And none of these fakers how it was last night.

They said they were locking.

We said, prove it, telepathic.

They drove from the high-ups and we said, how can you drive with your size mutating?

If you're locking that is.

You would shrink to a shrimp then swell to Godzilla.

Meaning the car would seem a monster truck. Then the car would seem a matchbox car.

How can you drive, we said telepathic.

And they couldn't hear us. Meaning they weren't locking but talk talk talk.

And we couldn't talk even. Proof we were locking. We couldn't walk even from mutating size and from stiffened limbs and soaring souls.

It's about motor coordination that it says on the bottles. Impaired in bold letters and potential narcosis.

We call it Bride of the Monster. Meaning Frankenstein's Bride.

But they don't read the bottles because what do they care? They never lock. And worse than that. They cram bottles in their shirts. We've witnessed their crimes. We've seen them stealing as in last night's stealing. Shirts crammed with bottles to shake us up. Stolen from our drugstore where we know the workers. That's our contention.

We always pay. We're the truest thing.

And with our lesser cash ask any.

Think of cooking funnel cake in the daytime. That's us.

Now think of serving ribs at night to high-rise high tippers. That's them.

So who's got the capital?

Not that we need more than lucky shells. We don't need cars and cash and all their whatnot.

And we moved to the ocean before any ask any. We moved in May and it was vacant in May before school let out. Before The Invasion.

And all through May we could feel the spirit. It felt like shhh like semi-spectral.

We said, we're sick of school! And, school hurts the spirit!

Jail, we said and, who needs jail?

Our mothers couldn't stop us. They tried to stop us with crying and whatnot like that would've stopped us.

Go back to school, they said. See a shrink, they said.

Ha. We would never.

You're kids, they said. We were caught alone in the shade-drawn room.

We're not, we said. We're the truest thing.

We took the three hour bus to the ocean.

And we invented locking in May. We had influenza from night swimming. The ocean degrees still dropped

like winter and we nursed each other from influenza
with sleep and whatnot. With doses of fire.

Meaning bottles and bottles.

And with this love we have.

Call it anything but gravity fell clear out. We saw
vivid lit tracers. Our souls took soaring to foreign lands
with circling moons.

Like being cold your whole life and a blanket appears.

And we said, what influenza? We're feeling healthful.

And locking is lawful so you can lock on the boardwalk without getting handcuffed. Even with the force
walking their circle.

It's completely lawful and we'll fight our fine.

We're first going to call a lawyer.

First off what did we do, we'll say. First off we
were at the arcade ask any. First off we didn't steal,
we'll say. Second we did nothing unlawful.

We were getting in touch and where is the crime?

We only do what's best for our life-way.

The force called our mothers. Thieves, they said.
Our mothers cried. They carried on.

We'll get you two!

We're not two, we said. We're one.

Should we prove it again?

Caught in the act in the matchbox room. Caught in
April in the shade-drawn room. Instead of school. How
two turns to one true love.

And we didn't stop when the light flew in. We didn't
cover up when she said, you're kids! And, I'm telling
his mother.

And we didn't stop when they tried to jail us.

We took the three hour bus. They never came looking.

The shrink maybe said, it's what kids do. They'll come creeping back.

Ha. We would never.

But the force said, come get them.

Our mothers cried, kids!

We're not kids we say.

We're souls with limbs.

Which is why we need to live at the ocean.

Though everyone's talking of a lower high-rise.

Next summer they say. Lower turns high-rise.

But we'll never let our lower get wrecked. We'd sooner stand in a wrecking ball's path and we've seen the machinery. Bulldozers. Whatnot.

And if we get cuffed for saving our cabin from being flattened just lock us up and toss the key.

It's proof we're soulful with true potential.

We're the only truth.

Last night in our cabin we drank a bottle. We were Frankenstein and Frankenstein's Bride. We walked to the boardwalk to lock.

These fakers were there for their last night of summer. Bright-lit eyes. Not locking but faking, wow man, like the sixties and, I'm sauced I'm sauced.

We would have laughed if we could.

They had stolen bottles crammed in their shirts. They said so even. Stolen from our drugstore to shake us up.

We went to an arcade instead.

In the arcade everything went whoosh whoosh. We witnessed a dazzling show ask any. The skeeballs and whatnot. The pinball machines.

We stuck at the walls hearing the songs. We couldn't sing but that's locking where the fire creeps how fire does and makes it shhh.

Besides. Words are useless. Names are useless. We were, hey what's your name, across the arcade and even these words came wrong the letters wrong-ordered like a foreign language. We laughed inside but it wouldn't come out. Just our ribs shook like coughing and our limbs turned stiffer. Our souls soared outer. We called it Night of the Living but that's not what we meant. We meant Living Dead because that's what we looked.

We eyed the skeeballs in triple vision.

Then we eyed each other.

We had lucky shells crammed in our pockets.

We tried skeeball but nothing. The pinball but nothing. Just our motor coordination truly impaired.

A thought of school came in went out as a sound of school then cool then ool.

We were locked into each other hard. We frenched by the wall.

A thought came in as a sound of love and it stayed as love.

We saw tracers streak in triple vision. We saw lit vistas. The fire sunk deeper into our heads. It got closer to sinking all the way. Our heads were fusing. Our souls took soaring to outer lands. Warm foreign lands of yellow moons. We spoke telepathic. But we weren't there yet.

Though we didn't want farthest.

As in once spirit turned to spit spit spit and the land turned to waterfalls crashing around us. There were blood-red moons. And we could see the void as syrup in the distance.

We both held on for the love of life.

We were close to dead.

It's a good thing we have each other and love.

Last night could have been our most dazzling lock.
The space between tracers and crystal lands.

It's a point of degrees. We spoke telepathic. Just
one more bottle. A critical dose.

We stuck to each other and zombie-walked.

These fakers stood on the boardwalk staring. In-
vading. They called their, far out. Their, wow.

We said, prove it, telepathic. We kept our souls
high.

In the drugstore our faculties were out of order.
We were Godzilla in the aisles wrecking the floors.
The lights chirped above. Our heads touched the lights.
We could feel them sparking. We could hear them
chirp against our ears.

We walked to the influenza aisle. We took a bottle
and looked for the workers but we couldn't find
them with triple vision. We were lost in the drugstore. And our ribs shook like coughing. Like inside
laughing. We opened the bottle. We drank the fire
and fast.

Then whoosh! Handcuffs.

And the workers shook their heads shame shame.

And we shrunk to shrimp. We curled in the wet by
their shoes.

We could see their faces as yellow moons.

Thieves, they said. Delinquents.

We were caught in the act of what we say.

The workers knew we would buy the bottle. They
knew we never once stole. We paid in cash every day
with our funnel cake cash.

And, keep the change, we often told them.

Just we couldn't get our faculties straight. We had
flown past critical. Entering crystal. The force circled
over as blood-red moons.

Delinquents. Thieves. The words turned foreign in our heads. The letters wrong-ordered. Our limbs locked up in rigor mortis. We crossed the street in monster-steps. The fakers stared. It was Night of the Zombies we looked so dead.

And we passed through crystal. We turned to see it dazzle in the distance.

We said telepathic, we'll call our lawyer. Sounding all chirp chirp. Like waterfalls. Like little birds.

And we monster-walked into spinning lights. Into almost void. Then, where are we going? And then, where are we? Where am I, as the fakers faded out. We faded out.

Our mothers came on the three hour bus. Their syrup faces. Vacant eyes. Their chirping chirping, you're going to school.

But they dropped out too. They had the sixties life-way. Far out and space. Free and true love.

But they sold their souls to the Land of the Lost.

Because of you kids!

We're not kids, we say.

We're the end of free love.

And what's worse is we can't see each other. We're in different spaces with weakened telepathy. Loosened limbs.

And now there's gravity.

And I'll tell you what's worse.

I'm Helen Keller only I'm not faking. I'm knocking into walls here like I'm impaired. Like I'm blind. I'm fused to the bed and I can't see the blankets. And I'll tell you what's worse.

I'm hearing through the window cars I know. These fakers' cars. They're back from the ocean for back to school. And I'll tell you worse.

I've drawn the shade in this matchbox room. I'm fused to the floor. It's getting harder and colder. Like the void. Like dead.

And my soul is wrecked.

And you sit there taking it.

Forward

April 14

Hello. My sister was hurt at your last game. Her injuries include one on her head and several scrapes. Please come see her at St. Vincent's. The visiting hours go late. We will keep it a secret. There are bruises on her knees. You could eat together. She has a pocket camera and wants a picture. You could pose on the bed.

April 15

Hello. My sister always prays for you to win. She is your biggest fan and I can prove it. She wishes on her eyelashes to meet you. Visit and help her break into the commercial scene. She knows exciting ways to pose and smile. One way for perfume and one way for underwear. My sister wants to do a commercial because first it will put her on TV. Second it will make her money. Third it will prove to the world she is living large. She has to wait for the stitches to come out. She lost her wallet. Please bring her something to eat. There is always yellow pudding and there is always peas and wet bread.

April 15
I will tell you. There are manholes you can slip down into. Inside is a separate world with tunnels. Down the right manhole is where the money is. Then there is love which is down the same hole. My sister can steal wallets so smooth. She came to New York to find her dream come true and she did. There was a TV close-up of you shooting. She had to steal money for the sequined evening gown and for tickets. I will tell you something. There are manholes that even famous you can fall clear through. Things are not sealed up tight. That is how airplanes explode. And how men peep through windows. You have to be careful or you will fall down wrong and end up hurt in St. Vincent's or worse. Jail.

April 16
My sister made a poster saying I LOVE YOU and everyone thought it was not a confession of true love but of a fan's deepest admiration. She wanted to end up on nationwide TV but she was sitting too far. Well she is building an important chair. It has collapsible legs. She can hide it under her evening gown. She wants to sit up higher so you will see her in the crowd. She will give you the peace sign and you will give her

the peace sign and she will wave her poster up high. New York will be jealous when she is higher up than anyone and screaming for you. Someone will hire her to make a thousand chairs. Then she will get a patent with her name on it and make a commercial. If you saw her chair you would ask for one and then she could give you hers and see your private locker room.

April 16

My sister is not jealous that the cheerleaders drop to their dirty knees and say they want to please you. They are hollow. My sister is the one who rushed down after a jealous player on New York elbowed you. She wanted to tear off her evening gown and hold it to your face. Let me just ask you. Did the cheerleaders offer help? New York fans say you are not generous but my sister says to look at your wrist and the ring of stars tattoo. When my sister thinks of you she thinks of the ring of stars tattoo and calls it your self-portrait. What is more giving than stars and also more bright?

April 16

I know you had to work extra hard for fame. And now look at you winning for your team! If you played for New York my sister would switch to them as her number one. Not because of your ring of stars tattoo. My sister saw you on nationwide TV in an exclusive interview. You give money to causes! My sister says, he is not an instigator! He is just misunderstood! She looks into your eyes when they give a close-up. You shake your head in disbelief when you miss a shot. You've had to work very hard. You sleep on your side all curled up in a ball like the rest.

April 16
My sister would like to be a cheerleader. She is blonde and has true spirit. She can do different kicks and splits.

April 17
The enemies are the New York fans who yell and spill drinks on my sister. And the nurses who flap around like big crows. And the nurses' cold hands and their needles. And this tray of wet yellow-brown. One nurse flashed a white light in my sister's face. They are stealing her personal mail. I secretly hand her letters to the man who brings the food. My sister wants your personal address. She does not trust this care of so and so one. My sister's injuries include a fracture.

April 17
Some lies my sister heard. That you will never play for New York. That you are still letting the cheerleaders drop to their dirty knees. That someone else is your biggest fan. These are lies made up by New York fans! You can understand my sister's fear when someone says you are out of her reach. Let's prove them wrong! Ignore all letters from anyone else. They are sent by liars who will say my sister does not even exist. It was one of these liars who hurt her so she would not get to meet you after the game. Well she is going home as soon as her head feels better and you are running out of time to visit. A visit will clean up your name.

April 18
Guess what. Well I will tell you. My sister dreamed she saw you in a restaurant and you said, hey love what's that color of your hair, and she said, Miss Clairol

ash, and you said, it looks like the sun, and slapped her good with the biggest hand she had ever seen. They gave my sister a sleeping drug to take through a needle at night. It brings you here as a hazy angel on the ceiling. You feed my sister strawberries on the roof of a skyscraper. You open up a fire hydrant and cool off in the street. My sister has a ring of stars pen-drawn on her wrist. She will need some time to prepare herself for you. The tubes tangled up her hair.

April 18
My sister feels she owes you something for interrupting the game. She got a little wild. And believe me she is paying for it with her throbbing headache. My sister wore white sneakers under her evening gown so she could run to the court faster at the end of the game. She knows this goes against fashion. I hope you are not making fun. Think about this. She gets cold drinks poured on her as a result of being your biggest fan. It is freezing when this happens. And now look who is broken down in St. Vincent's.

April 18
When you stormed off to the locker room at the end of the game my sister ran after you and tapped you with a five dollar bill with her number on it and she thought you said something like, watch it love, but then she thought you said, I'm not your fucking dancer. Which was it?

April 18
Hello. My sister was seeing stars from the injuries but she made it to your hotel. Her fancy evening gown was torn and bloodstained from the fight that started

after a liar called my sister something dirty. She was just cheering for you so hard and the New York fans would not let her express herself. She went crazy waiting so long for you. Were you at a certain cheerleader's house? My sister should have cleaned herself better but she could not stop the blood. She had several cuts and scrapes. She sent a note to your room and curled up behind a plant.

April 18
There is a manhole you can slip down into. You will go through a tunnel to my sister's room. How much does her head have to throb? My sister has several infections from not taking the medicine. She is on a starvation diet until you visit. She snapped some exciting pictures of herself. It will enhance your fame and benefit both of you to visit. Your enemies will swallow their words. My sister has ambition. She is cheerleader material. Look where she is—New York where she can break into the scene. You should switch your team to New York. I will tell you something. When my sister first got here to St. Vincent's she could only say your name over and over.

April 19
No mail today. Look for the city mail in the mouse hole. The nurses too. Then they crowd the room.

April 20
Guess what. Well I will tell you. The chair is good for everyone. You can be the commercial costar.

April 20
Hi there. It's me the head of the cheerleaders. I thought we could hook up again sometime soon. I'm in St.

Vincent's with multiple injuries. I'm in a flowing white hospital evening gown. I want to get down on my dirty knees and please you. Come over to play. My hair's brushed out all smooth and blonde.

April 20

Sorry to you and to the head cheerleader. I got a little wild. Blame the nurses. I said no crazy medicine that makes me forward. I owe you. I will tell you a secret. How to steal a wallet. But you have to come here first.

April

The nurses are so floaty today. And hundreds of them in a row. Ha. They zip. They go all out. Sponge me up and dry.

April 21

You hovered above me like a floppy angel or a helicopter. You gave me a pair of your shoes and I said, these are so big I could live in them! We held hands and you pulled me up. The nurses crawled into a mouse hole when we started spinning and I floated back to the bed like a feather. The nurses squeaked their rubber shoes outside the mouse hole to pour me water.

April 22

The needles keep getting bigger! Come visit so I can eat. I love the way you smile down on me. I love your sparkling wings. You hazy angel get me out of here. Remember I said that? Before we started spinning? Then I woke up sweating. And I will tell you something. I have made a few good moves.

April 22

Think about long ago when things sounded different. If you were to sit on an endless green lawn on a small chair or a blanket on a clear summer day and hear a string quartet playing a few feet away on a wooden platform there would not be a plane overhead or a car zooming by. Think about the faraway past and the green lawn and a string quartet playing a few feet away on a wooden platform and you can hear a violin sound pouring out. Imagine you hear this clear sound with no other outside sounds to break it up and you can ride on it. It soars in an arc. Now imagine a ball soaring through the air on this note. Do you understand this? It is profound! Imagine the clear uninterrupted violin sound streaming out over your head in an arc. Now imagine a ball soaring through the air on this sound. This is the ball when it leaves your hands. It sails through the air in an arc and the crowd is screaming and clapping soundlessly and there is only this lone violin sound streaming out. Your eyes are focused on the ball. You turn and walk away in slow motion. The room is silent except for the lone sound. The ball falls through the basket with a sigh then there is instant volume and everyone is caught up in the mess. Think about back when things sounded different. You know what I am getting at.

April 23

At last a big personal envelope. The nurses say, open it when you eat. I will write this for awhile and draw and then there is TV. It is about not jumping out of my skin. The nurses do not want me to open my stitches again. Here comes the man. There is another bite of bread. Another sip of juice. Another needle later.

Goodbye to the night nurse with her head pressed against the wall. The envelope smells like cologne. It is your personal scent. You can be the star of the commercial. I will pose on top of your head. Then a flash to your arms all flexed. Then me doing a dance and you can join in. Then a close-up of your self-portrait. Then the chair alone with some blinking lights and good music. Well. The envelope had my wallet inside. Get this ring of stars off me. She is up and here comes my shot.

April 24
From the mouse hole is a bright light under the door and the metal bed that is empty and no visitors allowed especially not you. Do not try any lurking near the windows. From down here the squeaky shoes and a dripping. Everything is clear green out of a slit here so do not come get me. It is time for the chair starting here with a plan. I will make a list. First the wood. Second a pillow. Third a hammer and nails. Then another fancy gown. Take this roll of film. I will build the chair high enough to poke you in the eyes. The New York fans will help me up. The cameras will find me floating up there like a bird and I will throw cold drinks at you from up high screaming, go New York! I love you New York!

TWO

Far

It started at the pond behind the highway. We
dangled from the branches of the trees. There were
crickets and frogs. We threw leaves at each other. I
ran through the shallow water or slept on the grass.
He had beautiful hands and crooked teeth. He chain-
smoked and drove an old police car with a siren that
worked. I stole things for him from stores. He waited
in other parts of the stores in case I got caught. He
waited at his apartment for a call from the police. He
waited in his car with the heat going. I slept on the
couch or on the bed. I gave him small gifts and left
them on the front seat of his car. They were stolen but
meaningful like once a small TV. Once a carton of

cigarettes. He put his hands tight around my neck and said, you're so.

You just want me to become famous. You know this will make you well-known like Freud. You will write a book about me and our sessions and then you will be living larger. You can read my mind when I twist in your chair. Open the window for me. Don't mind that I'm pulling leaves off the plant. I should tell you that behind your head I can see a man in the window across the alley. He's drinking tea out of a blue cup and he isn't wearing a shirt. He's distracting me. And it reminds me.

He lived off the highway. We sat in his old police car. He gave me the apartment keys. He said, I'll park the car somewhere. Go inside and wait. Listen to music. Turn on the TV if you like. I turned on a radio. I couldn't find the TV. In the medicine cabinet were broken thermometers. In the refrigerator nothing. There was a cat sleeping in a flowerpot. I waited on a kitchen chair. He came in and put me up on the counter. He had beautiful hands and crooked teeth. I felt my shoes slip off. Then everything else slipped off. At the pond he was drinking whiskey out of a bottle when he thought no one was looking. He said, what's your name again? He knew my name. He said, what's your favorite thing? I said, gravity. He said to someone else, her name's gravity. He put my finger in his mouth. I thought I could fly off then twisting up dust and leaves like a tornado. I thought if I waited I would be lifted by a flapping sound getting closer and closer to my head. The pond chased itself in circles. The air shuddered around my arms. The ground felt cool and I pushed my fingers into it. He said, what's your favorite thing? I said, you know it's TV. I meant to say, you're my favorite thing. That would have been a good answer but still I ended up with him. He wanted me even though there were other girls eyeing him. He said, come over here. He put his hands on my face. I said, do I taste like cigarettes? He said, you taste good. I said, what are we doing here? Shhhh.

In a dream you and I sat at a table in your house but it was my bedroom. You lit a cigarette off a candle. A man knocked at the door. He had teeth like a movie star. You pointed at the door and it looked like the end of the world. I said, why don't you let me stay? I walked outside and crossed a bridge into a dark yellow sky. In the sky I was running from the police. You were there too helping me get to safety. You can tell me what this means. When you dream about me I wonder if you're left with a hollowed-out feeling. I should tell you that many days have passed on the ceiling of my bedroom. I sleep or I eat and drink. I sleep the most.

He didn't answer the phone. I said, don't you want to get that? He said, no, and held me tighter. I said, is that the sun out there already? He held my arms above my head. I knew being with him was a step backward. His fingernails were too sharp. I didn't even know where the TV went. I wondered if he sold it. The room was warm. He unbuttoned my shirt to help me breathe. I thought, it could be worse. It could be that.

In a dream I cleaned your house with a feather duster. I wore a black lace apron. You watched me from a spiral staircase. A bat flew into my hair and got trapped. I rolled around on the rug trying to put out an invisible fire. You were having a cocktail party. I stood alone by the door. I sat in the corner of the couch. The flowers wilted around me. You drew a chalk line down the center of the room. You said, this is my side. That is your side. You confiscated my cigarettes. I said, I can't be here without them. If I could smoke in here there would be more to talk about. I wouldn't be so scrambling. I have to touch the plant and the dirt now. It feels good like I'm behind the highway. I should tell you I once wore a wig and dark glasses to the pond but he didn't notice and I started to think I wasn't wearing them but I could feel them. I should tell you in the waiting room I once put my face on the shoulder of your red coat. It smelled like snow and metal. It brought back memories that weren't even mine. The cover of a book about a family that lived in the mountains. I reached into your coat pocket and pulled out a grocery list. I put it in my wallet just in case.

I said, put the TV on. I can't be here without it. He said there was nothing on. I didn't even know where the TV went. He was worse off than I wanted him to be. Who taught him how to drink like that? He drank whiskey out of the bottle when he thought no one was looking. He pushed me down on the thin bed and I became air and dust. For a few minutes I circled out of my head and into his. This part gave me nice energy later. It felt like going under water and then breathing down there. I heard a sound like a helicopter. My veins all pushed a way to the top. I held on to his hands his hair his shirt. If I didn't I would have been swept up by a black cloud of birds and leaves. The bed helped to hold me down. I said, I saw you drinking whiskey out of the bottle you drunk. I said, what's *your* favorite thing? I said, I love your teeth. He asked me to stop talking. I said, they pick up the trash so early around here. He dragged me into the bathroom. I said, look at me. I looked at myself in the mirror. I said something. I said something else. I shouldn't have.

In a dream I saw you in the window across the alley. You were drinking tea out of a blue cup and the man was cutting a lemon. He pulled the shade up and down and up in some kind of secret code. I wonder why you were over there. I think you were drilling him. I should tell you you don't give the plants enough water. They're dying in here. Look the leaves are brown and limp.

From the bathroom floor I could see the window open in the other room. The curtain waved in and out. This was nice for awhile. I pulled broken mirror out of my arms. I could hear the traffic outside coming inside. I tried to get him to wake up. I whispered, I'm leaving. Wake up for a second. He was making no sense. In his sleep he told me to take the cat for a walk. The cat was nowhere in sight. The room was getting lighter. The shadows under his eyes made him look like an old man. I hadn't noticed that line around his mouth. I took his coat and left. I sat on the curb and looked at your grocery list. Who drinks the wine in your house? Don't tell me.

I walked through the alley where the trash cans were rolling on their sides. I walked on the highway where a few cars raced past. My neck was throbbing and my arms hurt. I walked by pumpkin stands. All the stores were closed. Sometimes I felt like I was running but it was the wind pushing. My shoes were half off. It was Saturday. The sun came up over the mountains. You would have laughed if you saw me. You would have said I took some control leaving like I did. My shirt was buttoned wrong. I had stolen his coat. The pond looked different with the sun out. I walked in the soft mud. My shoes were wet. There was a feeling like nothing. Then one like hunger. Then I was tired. Tired enough to sleep in the mud. In his coat pocket I found the keys to his old police car. My head fit perfectly in his hands you know. I could hear him whispering above me. He said, stay still. I thought, this is what the end of the world feels like at first. Then the hands release your neck and you float away like dust. I should tell you I want to be alone for awhile. You should be paying me. Ha. That's a good one. I need a break from you. You murdered all the plants.

The pond looked like a postcard with the sun out like that. Dogs chased sticks on the grass. I ran through the water splashing some birds. There were leaves in my hair. I slept under a tree.

THREE

Life

just me and him driving, just the road and road signs, just broken white lines on the road, just the headlights nearing, then past, then dark, just the radio hum, a song, what was it, just a song from before, just his untucked shirt, his coat on the seat, just my lipstick rising up and up, just my lipstick pressing to my lips in the dark, my: do you like it, his: do I what,

just me and him on the road, going fifty, going sixty, seventy, just the oncoming headlights' glow on his hair, then none, a luster, then dark, a luster, then dark, just me looking through the windshield, just broken white lines in the road like stars, just flashing below us as we straddled the lines, and we were flying through space, over space, it felt that, just the radio humming, just the rocket-sound motor, just my lipstick curved in a hook and rising, my: what do you think, his: what do you mean,

just his looking at me looking to the road, and seeing me as a luster then dark, and seeing my head nodding out just a song, a song from the party, and there had been liquor, no, none for me, just a clear head for me, just my clearest thoughts, as I often thought these clear dirty thoughts, not like hazy dreams of I don't remember, but more like daydreams, crystal, in bed awake, traffic glowing and fading on the ceiling, and he does what he does in my head, as do I,

just his zipper spreading, just his face not knowing what to think, just his foot pressing down and down and down on the pedal, and I thought, split second, just that it's a free world, just that we're dust and water, and the universe, that vast vast hole, well,

just we'd been dancing, not close, just swaying at the party, just I fell into his dance, his sway, and we swayed in a circle, just the liquor smoke taste on his tongue, well I hadn't yet tasted it, just the sweat on his forehead, and I hadn't yet felt it, and I thought, what if, and I thought, watch the road, just watch the road, and, don't look down at me, and, don't look up, just I

thought that to myself, don't look up, and, keep your
eyes shut tight, and I tried to do just that,

just I couldn't stop thinking of what if what if, and
of what if I didn't, just I was twenty-what, over twenty,
getting older and older, closer to what was it, the vast
outerworld, and the dark to luster made his face an-
gelic, and I thought of my lips leaving lipstick prints,
just tokens of the night up his arms, down his legs,
just tokens for him to look at later in the bathroom, in
the closet, and I thought of his fingers deep caught in
my hair and, later, his tongue, and, later, well, either
he would or he wouldn't,

just the zipper spreading, just his: what are you
doing, just me going down and down and down in
the dark, just him loosening his pants, just tightening
his grip on my back, on my hair, just one hand in my
hair, one hand on the wheel, just his whispered words,
just under the music, the rocket-sound motor, were
they: I don't know, or: just don't stop, just lights from
somewhere on the dirt on the floor, just the salt dirt
taste, just my eyes shutting tight as his foot went deeper
into the dark light dark, as the car rushed through
traffic going eighty, going ninety, I could tell from the
pressing of his foot to the pedal as I opened my eyes,
as my head jerked up, there was hardly traffic but
road signs, a strip of endless white stars pushing under the car, his hand on my head, my head going
back down, and down, and I thought to myself, shut
your eyes tight, and, this could be something like a
daydream,

just we'd been playing, just looking not looking, playing come and get it, and he said: what, and I said: I saw you, and he said: what, and I said: what, just it meant nothing anyway, just his eyes on my lips, and I thought of his girlfriend, her thin slit lips, just her lips were set in a thin tight line, just she was just that, a line, straight as a road, waiting for him to come home,

I waited after the party in the room with the coats, I waited in the bathroom, on the grass, by his car, and he said: do you want a ride or something, and I said: yes or something, just I needed a ride, just there was life the next morning and I needed to leave, I needed to sleep and a ride up the road, just up a few roads, it was getting late and he knew where I lived, just we'd known each other for years and years, same friends, same world, same lives all of dust and water and soaring outward at the same blink speed,

just knowing is not always knowing,

just we'd been dancing, just swaying at the party, and I thought, what if,

just we'd been looking not looking all night, just playing come and get me, come and get me, what if, just his foot pressed all the way down on the pedal and I wondered how fast that meant,

just blame him, it was all his fault,

just my head in his lap like a pet, and I could have stayed there and died there, his hands in my hair, petting my head, just the windows rolled down and the ice air from some distance from outer, from stars, from dead as dirt worlds, just seeing my house from far below and feeling made of dust, settled, short-lived, just his: see you later,

and opening the car door I was thinking of his girlfriend waiting at home, waiting to touch his already warm hands and his already warm cock and his already sweat-slicked forehead and his tongue tasting of smoke, or liquor, or lipstick, and she would know there was something, meaning there was nothing,

and later caught up in the ceiling I was thinking of all the sunlike stars in the universe and I was thinking of all the earthlike planets in the universe, and doesn't that mean something, all that potential, just that we live in a vast vast hole, just that we're moving outward in a flash, just that twenty-what is really twenty-nine and twenty-nine is really thirty and thirty-nine is really forty and seventy is ninety, just that there is life beyond life, almost always beyond reach,

Winner

1.

A toast to the new man and wife. Hear hear. To my
first friend forever. I'll cry I swear it. First friends for
life. From Girl Scouts onward. I swear we've been
through it all. So I knew she was devoted. I could tell
how she spoke. Like he was her only. Like he was her
brightest star in the sky I knew it I swear. And I could
tell his devotion. The way he looked her deep but off
to the side. So struck with devotion he couldn't look
straight. And I'm why they met. I made her go to the
party at his house. Heard from the grapevine. I said,
let's go. And, blank it all! Blank your work! Next thing
we dressed. Next thing our hair. Next in we walked.

There he was. There she was. All I can say is you could feel the spark. Like a spray of starshine shot from the walls. And I walked home alone that night I did. And they had their time in the woods. Then another. Then another. Their kissing and whatnot. Their spark. Wink wink. All star-struck. Soul-mates. In la la I remember. It was crazy how she got. How she banged into walls. How she skipped her classes. How she tracked pine needles all over the room. And I once saw her spray perfume into her mouth. That's something you never forget. Someone struck with devotion. Stars in her eyes. Making her parents worried sick. And I said, she's fine she's fine, to her parents. Just devoted, I thought. I kept that to myself. Though devoted she was. I knew it. She knew it. And he was devoted. Though after a few days he sort of let up. He sort of stopped calling. I remember when he stopped his calls. How she slept with the phone that week I swear it. Now that's true devotion. She called him each night all night. And always one of his brothers would answer. And always she'd be put on hold. She'd be sitting there sitting there sitting there. And I could hear sounds from the phone like a party. And I could see her in the dark from across the small room. Like a hotel room this room and I could see her clear. Her face lit green from the phone. And when they talked at last she'd get this look like all la la. She thought I wasn't looking. She thought I wasn't listening. But I heard their talks. How could I not? Our room was like a hotel room. Two beds. A bath. No place to walk. Her parents called it quaint. Remember how they said, how quaint. Remember how they cried when they left you? How they carried on sick with worry? And I said, let her go. She'll be fine. And you were weren't you?

In that small as anything room I swear. How could I not hear every single word? And she tried to whisper but I heard every single night, I miss you honey. Do you miss me honey? I love you honey. Do you love me honey? Look everyone. She's turning scarlet. That's true devotion turning scarlet. Can we see each other? I miss you honey. Can I see you tonight? And, let me please. It was sickening. She's scarlet. Look at her face. Sick with true devotion. And he said, no you can't. I'm busy tonight. You can't come over. I could hear it faint. And she'd cry in her blankets. She'd say, he's stringing me along. And I'd turn on the light. I'd say not to cry. I'd say he was busy with the frat house and not to cry. And blank him anyway. He was in charge of the frat house and overworked. He wasn't stringing anyone anywhere. And what would she do in the house anyway? Get bored by that boy stuff. That's all. The brothers and all. I'd say he was protecting her from the brothers. True devotion I'd say. Protecting her from the frat and those boys we'd heard about. The grapevine told us how they got at night. How they rocked each other. And she said, what do you mean rocked? And I said, like at Girl Scout sleepovers. Short-sheeted beds. Rocked you know. Toothpaste in the hair. Wink wink. Better to stay in the room, I'd say. You don't blanking need those boys. And we'd talk instead. Long deep talks about the past. How in Girl Scouts we did some crazy things. And we'd talk about the future. About graduating together and then working at the same place. And we'd get married at the same time. I could tell when she'd start thinking straight. She'd stop calling him. Like once for days she didn't call. I was proud of her. And sure enough one night ring ring ring I swear it. And she wouldn't take his call. And

next thing there he was at the door. And she said,
don't let him in, though he banged and banged. She
said, go away. And the next night was the same and
the next night and the next. How he called up beg-
ging. Slam! in his ear. How he showed up with flowers. A door in his face. I was waked every night with
the ring ring ring. Then bang bang bang. And it was
almost fun. Exciting. But it got her down I swear. She
skipped all her classes. All her schoolwork. She stopped
eating and washing I swear it. She just curled in bed
crying. And I heard her talking to herself. Not to me.
She'd hit rock bottom. And I heard her tell her parents, I'm fine I am, before curling in bed. Before talking to herself. Just in la la I thought. And he was too.
I saw him in the daytime seeming down. I saw him
bang his fist into a brick wall I swear it. Blood sprayed
out all over the wall. That you can't forget. And he
cried into the wall. I won't forget that. And then one
night the grapevine warned us. Watch out, it said. He's
in a mood. Something happened with his father or
something. Something big, I told her. Exciting. But
not in a good way. And next thing you know he kicked
in the door. Next we stood there startled. He dragged
by her hair I swear it. I'll never forget. It was finals
week and I jumped into bed. I pulled the blankets
over my face. Next thing all that screaming. I looked.
And his face was purple I swear it. And he was holding her over one arm like a rag-doll. All I can say is
devotion will do that. Devotion will let this happen.
Devotion is why he dragged her away. I slept well
that night. Dreams of running through woods but not
for long. She came back the next morning. The room
was still dark. And she was all messed up. Dirty. Dirt
on her clothes and pine needles. And she said, we're

getting married. And her eyes were bloodshot and she had twigs in her hair and I was like, are you sure? I hadn't even brushed my teeth yet. And she looked me straight and said, what do you mean am I sure? And I don't know what I meant. Just perhaps that marriage is such a big thing. And perhaps that finals were here. And what about our futures together our children together? She seemed suddenly so old or scarred. I couldn't decide. It seemed so rushed. But your parents, I said. Blank them, she said. I'm getting married this summer. It was so unlike her but to each his own. It was true devotion. And I gave my blessing and pulled twigs from her hair. I ran a perfumed bath. And here I am today on this lovely summer day. The most honored maid of honor. I could cry I could. Here come the tears. Of course I gave my blessing. I mean I'm why they met. And she's really devoted. Can't you feel the spark? Can't you tell they're soul-mates? Why else would someone skip finals? Why else would someone leave school? Why else would someone leave her first friend forever? Her family forever? For devotion that's all.

3.

A toast to the two. The classiest act.

A class act this guy. A winner.

The first one awake. The one to start cleanup. The rest of us sleeping it off. And I mean sleeping it off. The sun barely up. And he had the coffee on the eggs cooked the windows open wide. Even in the dead of winter. Up and at 'em! Up and at 'em! Screaming through the house. Banging pots and pans. Even on the deadest weekends. He had us up and at 'em crazy bastard.

He rocked us good.

I knew this guy when. That's all I'm saying. I knew him when. Freshman year. We were friends through it all. You know we were. Rush. Hazing. Fall madness. Spring fling.

We were the best of brothers. Two crazy kooks.

And now he's a class act manager. Promoted to management. And a married man.

If your old man could see you today. He'd be like. Well you know.

But honest. Let's just say we went through it all. The good times and bad.

I'll tell you something.

This guy. A class act. A winner.

Three hundred sit ups every morning. Three hundred push ups every morning. Three hundred chin ups and we'd be looking at him like, crazy bastard. We were so spent and the things this guy. The things I can't tell you. Honest. He'd kill me. You know it. The hazing ideas were all his. Go Greek! But I can't tell you. He'd rock me hard.

How many times was I like, man you can't do that. And he rocked me hard.

That kook.

Just kidding.

He was best man in the house. I'll start with that. Devoted to the house. It's an honor to be best man of the really best man.

You know what I'm saying. What I mean by best.

The ladies loved him.

No offense to the bride. He's all yours now Mrs. But he had his fans. Let's be honest kids. How many times was I like, brother friend. Share the wealth.

Ladies lining up for this guy.

But honest. When she walked into the house I knew. It was spring fling time. Am I right kids? Spring fling. Everyone crazy. No work getting done. In she walked. Picture this. Sophomore. That hair. Those jeans. That face. And that trophy body.

A living doll.

Can you hear me okay in the back?

He was all you know. And she was looking and looking.

We had a moment like brothers. I knew. He knew.

I said, brother she's the Mrs. But I didn't mean Mrs. I meant she's yours. Like to go out with or something. Like to be with in the woods.

I said, she's yours man.

I could tell the way she looked. It was like this. Come hither.

Am I right kids?

Come hither.

And he almost went the other way. There was this other little number. Honest. Her little friend. Her maid of honor. I saw him looking that kook. But does it matter? It doesn't now. What matters is he chose the blonde trophy. Hot body. He walked right up.

And that's all she wrote ladies and germs.

True love am I right?

I knew it. He knew it.

The way she called every night. Talk about your devoted. What do you want, he'd say. Honey honey, he'd say. He always found the time to talk. I mean even with his busy busy. He was in charge of this in charge of that. And pile on cleaning. Pile on push ups sit ups chin ups. Pile on pledges. Devoted to his brothers.

Overworked is right.

Your father would be proud man. I know he would. You'd make him proud.

A college graduate. Promoted to management. And a married man.

A class act brother. A winner. And this is about brotherhood. That's why I'm here today. The truest brotherhood. Fellowship. The Greek way of life.

And he is the truest brother.

The hazing ideas were all his. The whole thing with the water. The jump from the bridge. The underwater. The run through the woods. The run through mud and shit. He rocked them all. The one with the freshmen. Even the girls. Yes sir! Yes sir! He made everyone say it. Yes sir. Yes sir.

Well I wasn't saying it.

I said, brother man. I'm your brother. He looked me straight and said, you're my brother.

I still am man. Don't forget it. I always have been.

Like when his old man finally passed. The whole house came together as a whole. We were there together. Finals week. Graduation. The house was a mess. He was a mess. All week I was, man you can't do that. About this about that. What a week that week. He could've hit rock. But he was like, but I can.

Even though I said, you kook. You can't.

He rocked me good.

We were the best Greek brothers.

We threw some punches but we talked it out.

We went through the bad but we came out good.

I said, what's the hurry?

He rocked me hard.

I was so spent and I said, to each his own brother. That's what I said. And, go Greek brother!

And he dragged his girl to the woods.

All she wrote.

And here we are.

He paid for this whole wedding. Did you know that kids? A class act wedding. He paid for it all with his own hard cash. He's a class act manager.

And that's the kind of power he put in us all. I can. I can. I can.

Well yes sir!

If your old man could see you today. He'd be like. Crazy kook. He'd rock you good. You know what I mean.

Only kidding you kook. Only kidding brother.

A few last words.

Graduation day. Families sent home. Yes sir! Girl-friends sent home. Yes sir! Nighttime. Party. Freshmen girls. Yes sir! The house. The bridge. The woods.

All she wrote.

Drink up ladies and germs.

6.

Lucky you. You've tied the knot. Is that how you say it? The knot?

It sounds funny to say and stupid.

We fought all the time growing up as kids. Did he tell you this?

But somehow we're closer. I feel a bond with my brother. Like we tied our own knot.

Does that make sense?

I guess I see it the knot. Like we're tighter. Like we're tangled up in something. Like in string.

You know I thought I'd marry first.

Men were lining up for me. Beating a path to the door.

I had my fans.

And I had a man for a long long time. Like years was it? Like months? And he would have married me I remember.

Hard to believe this whole great day. The summer weather. Like dad's up there making it perfect.

Does that sound stupid to say or wrong?

I wrote some things. My memory you've heard.

Dad left us with these words. Always. Grab. What. You. Want.

Isn't that how it went what he said?

And my brother grabbed school. He grabbed the frat. He always wanted brothers.

And he grabbed you too. Lucky girl.

That's power in a way.

And he was always very clean and neat. And you look very clean and neat.

That's a person who gets somewhere. I'm the kind getting nowhere fast. Isn't that what dad said? Nowhere fast?

I didn't grab school and look at me. Plus I'm not very neat am I? I'm no Girl Scout am I?

I wrote some things. My memory you've heard.

My brother's a manager. I don't know these things. No one tells me. But he'll make the cash. He always finds a way.

He paid for this whole day even. I mean my mom couldn't afford it. And your parents are like MIA.

Missing. In. Action.

So my brother cracked out the cash.

Enterprising is I think the word.

You're looking at me funny. Did I say that wrong? Enterprising.

Wait. I'm remembering something.

We had a lot of funny times as kids. House wars. Yard wars. Mud and leaf forts. And runs with the dogs through the woods. We had all these dogs. Like three was it? I can't remember their names now. They're gone now.

And all those fights in the yard over things. Like over toys and games and deep talks we had. And that time he cracked my face with his fist.

What a summer day that was. I was sunning. He was tearing down the dogs' house. We didn't have any dogs left it was.

He remembers that crazy summer right? It seems just recent.

I guess it was. I mean I was engaged to be married that summer and that was just recent. Just last summer.

I can't remember who I was going to marry. Some blonde trophy. Hot body.

Soon I'll have my fans again. Lining up. Beating down the door.

Don't you think I look good? The scars are fading. Ask my brother.

What was he thinking with that pow pow pow? That kook. I was just sunning. I was just staring off into space. Into la la la.

I said something to him about getting married. I'm getting married.

And he was like, no you're not either.

But I had a long term man with a name. A trophy. I said, I'm getting married.

Then pow pow.

I'm not done yet.

Lucky dad that day. He was unconscious with sickness. He would have killed him. Meaning dad would have killed my brother.

Lucky dad missed that day in the yard. What a knot on my forehead. My cracked up face. He would have told me to grab what I could.

But I was going nowhere fast. My eyes were shot with blood. Or I would have grabbed my brother's face. And I would have torn it clean off his head. And I would have swung it around and swung it around and stomped it stomped it stomped it to a pulp in the yard.

Like dirt. Like shit or something.

But I was all dazed anyway. Those were some crazy swipes with his fist. Both fists. And his fingers were turning red.

Mom remembers the things I was saying.

Something like, you crazy fucker.

I'm no Girl Scout you know.

I was rock bottom but never unconscious.

And now we have this bond. Me and my brother. We're closer now tied up in string.

Wait.

I remember our funny times. Mud and leaf forts. Runs with the dogs through the yard.

I'm not done yet.

What did they say? Rocked did they say? Well he rocked me good. My brother rocked me into the sun.

And I was bandaged up in strings. Messed up.

Did he tell you that he rocked me?

Did he tell you about the flowers?

How when I was recouping he brought me flowers? Now that's sweet. It was my whole face shattered when he cracked my face. And he brought such lovely flowers and cried and cried by my bed in that small room. Like a hotel room only darker. And it looked like four of him there. And I cried and it felt like a stinging.

That's something you never forget.

Like hot needles swimming through your face.

Like me and dad on the same floor. Some crazy unit. And we couldn't see each other because of my blood.

We never did see each other. This took a long time to heal. I mean look at me here. It's been over a year.

A summer. A fall. A winter. A spring. And now summer again.

And I'm still healing.

But it's water below the bridge now.

Is that how you say it? You're looking at me funny. Water below the bridge right?

And my brother gave these purple flowers. Or my mom did. Well someone did. I don't remember. But they were pretty. Purple and green. Mom do you remember who brought me flowers mom?

She's choked up over there. Don't look at my mom.

Maybe it wasn't him with the flowers.

Lucky anyway he went back to school. Senior year. Graduation. We were so proud of him we were.

I was like MIA all year but I made it to graduation didn't I? Proud as anything right? Just me and my scarred up face. And mom. Front row.

Mom's getting choked up. Look at her choked up. I'm not done yet.

Dad always said, get married. Be a man. Get married. Be a man. Get married. Be a man.

And my brother said, I'm getting married. Right on graduation day he said this.

And it still hurt to cry. A year later it still hurt like needles. And mom drove me home and we were alone crying all choked up. And dad was gone. It was just recent. Like weeks.

Weddings can be hard on mothers. Especially with dad MIA.

But we're managing fine.

Me. My mother.

I remember something.

Dad always said, take care of your sister. Take care of your mother.

Well what do you know dad. He did. He did. He did.

Are you listening up there you crazy kook?

We're managing fine. We have a tangled up bond. Like string.

And I do look better. Ask my brother. My face healed up nice. My pretty face. Maybe I can find another long term trophy. One who doesn't mind scarred for life. Nowhere fast.

Just kidding you know. I'll manage.

I believe in marriage. I believe in devotion.

I'm so proud of my brother I am. He's going to make a perfect husband and perfect dad. Lucky you. I can just see it.

You know what I mean. Perfect. Like dad.

Wait. I'm not done.

I remember something.

There's a window.

Once he said, I've got a good one.

What's got four feet and cries?

Don't remind him. These old thoughts flash.

Once he said, I have a trick. He peeled an orange with his teeth.

Just don't. These crazy old flashes. Don't give him an earful but say, you're fine mister. And this is not lying. It is good to tell him when he does good.

For instance he sends oranges and the oranges turned up.

For instance he calls. This day. Each year. But not this once big deal. Though the phone rang early. The cat jumped and ran and the doctors were nice. They had good humor. They swore to put the phone to his ear.

So call, they said. Try midmorning.

And his voice will shake, they said. Expect it.

It was dark but now is lighter. The cat sits on the windowsill and there is sun past the window and mountains. And there is need for some quiet. A need to look at the mountains.

But the phone started up. It just rings and rings and the cat starts in.

Now is midmorning.

What a rough night before and perhaps there are pills. One would expect it.

One knows they have taken his transistor radio. They have taken his wallet.

One would expect restraint. A stupor of sorts.

Perhaps wait then. Perhaps call midday when his pills fade out.

Then he will talk. Then he will joke to ease it all and who doesn't love a joke?

Say, I've heard words from the doctors mister. Still I think you're sharp.

He will say, liar.

Say, still I think you're funny.

In the car he chewed orange peels. A trick for a laugh and he laughed his head off.

In the house he scratched a notch in the doorway. Stand straight, he said and, under five feet.

What does that mean?

Four feet it means.

And that?

You're a cat it means. Cats have four feet.

All for a laugh and he laughed and fell over. These old thoughts flash at the worst. His curling on the floor. Her tearing her hair. Crazy old flashes from the place in between. Not north not south.

The doctors said, we tried to feed him. He threw his food.

Oh for the love of. He's being funny!

They laughed and laughed.

Perhaps he will joke midday. Laugh when he does. Say, that was a good one.

And, grab the world with both hands.

One day he can come north. Swear it. Tell him there are evergreens everywhere. Has he ever seen real raccoons? They circle the trees and there's a sunset from one mountain red on the low clouds. Tell him, we could drive up to see it and the road twists in a way.

But he would fool with his radio. There are old-time shows.

Say, we could make a day of it.

And if he is up to joking be sure to laugh the way your mother could not. She could never as he could not be stopped once he got started. She screamed out her veins. She tore out her hair and crouched in a corner. Who in the good world could live with such joking?

Your mother said, worthless, and changed the locks. She unplugged the phone.

He moved to a room then he moved to the south.

And the south is known for sun.

The north is known for snow but there is sun past the window. The mountains in between. The cat on the sill. So call before dark and say, thanks for the oranges. What a shock each year. In the snow comes the mailman bent under a crate.

Say, I heard him today. I heard the crate land.

And, I would have called.

He has called each year and so what this once. He had a night and the doctors were good to call so early. To call in his place while he sat in a stupor.

We found your number, they said, in his wallet.

They said the wallet of a mister so and so.

Yes I know him.

They said, good thing we got you.

Good thing yes, and the cat ran through the dark. Now he needs to be fed. Oh for the love of. Feed your old self!

But you can't teach an old cat new tricks.

This is a good one. He will laugh and laugh. Remember this one. And the good ones from early.

They said, he had been sleeping in his car.

Well good thing it's warm down south!

That was a good one and everyone laughed.

They said, who knows for how long? Days? Weeks?

Well perhaps he's been tired!

It went on and on.

Then a flash of him there. A flash of the bed. Restraints. The backless gown. His poor arms poked through with tubes.

They said, here's what happened.

And you: I have to split now.

Before the particulars.

You: I'll call midmorning.

He will laugh at the good ones. The old cat. New tricks. Warm in the south. Who isn't tired?

Say, get out of there mister! There's a whole world!

And he will joke: a hole in the world.

Get out while you can.

They said, soon, and they will hand him his clothes. His torn overcoat. He is wearing it still in such heat.

And they will give it back with his car keys and comb. They have his underwear too. His wallet. His radio.

They will pat his back and send him outside.

He said, no one gets younger. The sun keeps you going.

And, the south is known for what looks like sun.

And, can you think of something that looks like sun?

No.

Try.

Lemons.

He moved to a room then he drove to the south. The answer was oranges. A funny flash of all these flashes.

He waves to the traffic. He combs flat his hair. The sun makes him sweat through the coat.

What good is a wallet if you have no money?

The radio feeds him jokes and he laughs his head off.

What good are particulars?

Big deal there are palm trees. Here are evergreens. Here is snow.

Mail money with a note saying, take it, and mean it. Don't forget who once paid for clothes.

Say, put the money in a safe place. Are your pockets sewn?

Don't forget who pays for oranges and mail a note saying, looking good!

But crates of oranges are cheap in the south.

Don't forget the car rides how he chewed the orange peel and who didn't laugh?

But that was far back. An age close to zero. Under five feet.

Don't forget he calls this day each year to say, happy thirteen. He says, I've got a good one, and they go on and on and don't think of his coat in the heat and of where he sleeps where he washes and there are sounds of traffic and you have to think his coat has been sewn by someone down south so that he is not alone so that the coat is no longer torn because if it is. Well.

Every year it is hard to say, wrong age, and, wrong everything mister.

I'm fourteen. I'm sixteen. I'm eighteen.

And he will call next year with a run of jokes and a happy thirteen. He just missed this year so what the oranges arrived and oranges will arrive next year and again as they did today.

Call and say, we could split one.

Tell him, get better, and, get in the car.

That same old car with the rusted out bottom. The same radio playing old-time shows.

Tell him, drive to the north.

He could live in the north with a new overcoat and there are doctors up north and they will listen and say, you're fine mister.

And he will say, but it hurts when I do this.

And what will they say?

They will say, if it hurts don't do it.

Doctors are funny. They scared the cat calling so early. What a shock when he jumped. He ran through the room.

They said, he's a mess. A call will do him good.

A call to say: what do they mean by mess? Wash up!

A joke.

A call to say: the oranges arrived today in a crate.

And, don't worry about me and I won't about you.

There is need for some quiet.

Say, it's hard to get oranges in north in winter. The raccoons eat the peels and even the seeds. Isn't that funny?

And he never thought it.

Say, they chew up the seeds! And, why didn't you?

He will laugh his head off. Or else will he cry. He chewed the peel but spit the seeds from the car.

What does that mean?

Raccoons have more humor.

He will say, I've got a good one.

And then, are you listening?

And then, are you there?

And be there for the run of jokes. Be there to laugh the way your mother could never.

What's got four feet and cries?

He curled on the floor. Your mother grabbed her hair. She pulled.

What then! What!

The answer: you.

And laugh. A laugh will do him good.

Soon, they said.

The radio plays an old-time show. He laughs at the jokes and waves to the traffic. The doctors watch through the window. They stare at his coat collar turned under at the missing buttons at the bottom unraveled as he waves to the traffic. They laugh at him standing poor mister the money you sent falling out from the pocket and what can you do but it is far from here. One good thing. The overcoat the radio all the way in the south where there is heat.

And it all comes back once a year with the oranges.

And it leaves as you open the crate.

And it comes back once a year with the call the same day: did you get the oranges? He wants to know and don't picture him walking up the house steps in the place in between. Not north not south.

And it leaves when you throw oranges from the door and they burst in the snow for the raccoons but he calls: did you get them? And it comes back and don't picture him as he stands at the door in his overcoat and it is too cold for such a thin coat and he says, how are you Sweetie? And you say, fine, and he says, don't lie, and he is living in a room you never saw and his ear is plugged with the radio and there is a present in one of the coat pockets. He says, reach in, and in one pocket is a hole and in the other a small cat for your birthday. Since you're a cat, he says and, happy thirteen, and you are thirteen though the cat is not real but a toy and he says, I better leave now. He is sweating in winter. In the car are boxes. He says, here comes your mother and I better make like a tree.

Do you get it?

And leave.

And good thing laughing dragging to his rusted car and he waved big deal as you were pulled from the door and he drove to the south.

Your mother said, worthless. The door slammed shut. The toy got tossed from the window.

And there were thoughts of the north. Crazy flashes of running upward.

What's in the north?

Nothing.

That's where I'll go then.

When you're a grown up.

The phone ring rings and what then what? It is midday already. Time to call.

But the phone is ringing.

When the phone stops call him and for once say, thank you. And, I'm thirteen. And, I love oranges!

Say, how could you peel the skin with your teeth?

Say, how could you I wonder.

And, I have a real cat. He's named after you. I wish he would learn.

And, say his name and I will hold the phone to his ear.

And, you're looking good mister. Trust me on this. I can see your good looks.

He will like this joke. He will say, you lie.

Say, you're the sharpest.

He will say, liar.

Say, I'm over five feet.

He will say, how do you walk with over five feet?

Say, I have a cat. He's named after you.

And he: I don't like the food.

And you: you have to eat.

And he: it's salty and shouldn't be.

And you: I have this real cat. He's orange and I have named him after you. He doesn't know his name and he needs to eat but I can't get up from bed. I can't get up to help. And he'll never learn. I can't quite pull up today and the oranges are outside. I heard the mailman and I heard the crate fall but I can't quite get up to see the oranges. And they always make a mess and I can't feed the raccoons and I can't feed the cat and the cat can't feed himself. Do you know why this is?

And, if you call the cat he won't run to you. Call him your name and he won't run. Do you know why? Guess why.

You can't teach an old cat tricks!

He will laugh hard and as he laughs say, look how lovely. See the sun out your window?

But there are implications.

Say, don't do it again. You really don't want to.

But he does. Otherwise why did he try?

Say, we should talk sometime.

But this is a talk.

Say, we should visit together.

But this is a visit

Or, you messed up mister.

But that would be mean. Or that would be funny. A funny joke.

Or just, no!

Could you say this?

Or just, I've got a good one. Are you there father?

And laugh laugh laugh.

That was a joke and no one laughed.

Say, did you hear what I said? Did you hear my joke? Or is the radio plugged in both ears?

He will say, this food's terrible.

This is a joke.

He will say, the recipe calls for a dash of salt.

And he will say, how does it end?

He will say, tell me! How does it end?

Say, I thought it said a dish of salt!

And laugh.

And he will say, I won't do it again. I won't I swear.

This is a joke.

They will hand back his coat and comb. His radio and wallet. The rest of his pills or was it even pills or was it a rope or a razor or a window high up? What is the difference? A rope a razor. What does it matter? These are particulars. There's a window where he is. It looks out to the sun so tell the doctors, push it open, because the sun keeps you going. Tell them, push it wide, because what is it to say, don't jump! Don't cut! Don't think! I'll visit!

What is it to say, I'm taller now, and notch the wall for a laugh? I was small then because of age only of age. Less than five feet remember? That's why I never called you. That's why I threw the toy. I've thrown the oranges. I've been small all these years but look. Over five feet.

You can't teach an old cat.

What is it to answer the phone? To pick it up mid-ring?

Your mother says, those worthless oranges.

What is it to say, let's drive up the mountain. Look at the sunset! And he fools with his radio and you say, unplug your ear. Give me your coat. Let me sew your worthless coat. And he hands it and the radio is in one pocket a hole in the other and he is cold and crumbling as the coat flies off the mountain.

Your mother says, happy happy.

And what is it to say into a crying face, you aren't a mess. You aren't a wash up. Your world can be turned upside and over. And you're looking good mister. Grab the world with two and listen to my good one. I'm making like a tree. A worthless tree. Do you get it? And splitting. There's a need to split now. There's a need for quiet. The sun has set and the cat needs to eat.

And today is my birthday and I am a grown up.

What is it to be grown up and still lying like a child?

FOUR

What Makes You Think

I'm fine.

Just I've been through it.

As in: do you want to see my scars? I'll show you scarring twining inside and out. I'll show you what Numbers One through Five did. How they pushed me into the world.

Such clutter.

It was all I could do not to sob.

And the world is made of crazy echoes. I say, listen-listen. It comes back. Listen-listen.

I once went into the world on Saturdays. My father

used to drive me. As in: he drove me to the shopping center. All those crazy shops. Crazy plants.

Airtight with no way to let sounds out.

In the shopping center that is.

Not in the car. I know what you're thinking.

My father drove me and my girlfriends. Swerving by cliffs to make my girlfriends scream. And all my girlfriends liked my father. And my father liked my girlfriends. The other fathers drove us home. It was almost dark by then. There were no cliffs the way home but almost quiet. Rustling bags.

My dreams are of cliffs when I sleep.

I've gotten sidetracked here in my chair.

I didn't exactly up and leave One through Five. I said, I'm-leaving, or some such and flew out for good. I can hear what you're thinking and you're thinking, hysteria.

My girlfriends were flashy. Knockout. They were dramatic. Together we flew off our rockers.

And now when I see them. Or the shopping center. As in: from in my headspace. Well small birds take flight from my gut to crash into my ribcage.

We had thoughts of driving off a cliff. Me and my girlfriends chattered. What-if-we? What-if-your-father? Would-your-scream-get-trapped-in-the-car? And we got closer and closer on the way to shop. My girlfriends screamed. My father drove a red car. I know you're thinking, flashy.

I can see what goes on in your headspace. Your whole big drama.

Like Number Two and her, me-me-me, and her daughter her husband her garden.

I didn't care. I don't now.

You're Number Six and what makes you think?

My dreams are of cliffs. I wake in a fright. And the shadows keep me awake.

As in: last night's shadow. Shaped like a man and I live alone. I was dreaming and just as the car went flying I waked. There was a man-shaped shadow until the sun came in. Then the shadow thinned and it was just from a chair I learned.

I'll tell you how my scars look. Like thin red dresses like my girlfriends' dresses. They twine from my neck to my knees.

Numbers One through Five could never imagine. They disrupted harmony. They infringed on the session. On my personal upwardness. The reason we're here. The reason of fixing my life.

It's all I can do not to think of those others. Those ones who come here. The strangers. Their fits. Their fat squeezed into my chair.

How they knock my chair aslant.

And trust me I've spoken words on the matter. To Number Three I gave a, what's-with-my-chair, as often trust me there was a slant of sorts. A view of the plants.

As in: utter hysteria on the part of some sobbing stranger. A shoe knocks my chair out of line. My chair is left wrong. Some crazy swivel.

But I never gave a, who-moved-my-chair? Or a, who-slanted-it?

I just counted to ten and slow.

You're thinking, why-should-anyone-go-through-this? I know it. The least part of the deal is a straight-on chair.

And once I did hit my ceiling. I gave a, put-it-the-way-it-should-be. Fix-it. Now! This all before I took off my coat. I turned my back on Number Four with a, put-it-right. I saw red. And I counted to ten. Slow. The way we're taught for utmost harmony.

And guess what.

I counted to ten slow and turned to see Number Four shrug of all things to see. An, I-don't-know-what-you-want-from-me. And of course my chair swiveled that same slanted way.

Imagine standing all day in tight shoes. Imagine all day standing just to walk in from long hard hours to think, wait. Something-is-different. Then, solved! My-chair-is-wrong.

Needless to say I'm still significantly flustered. I'm still reeling off my rocker.

Once I found a shopping bag in my father's car. It was under his seat. My girlfriends were screaming as he neared the cliffs. I reached into the bag.

I'm sure it rustled.

Forget the sidetrack.

I said to Numbers Three and Four, leave-my-chair-as-is. And, tell-your-others. And, if-not-I'm-leaving.

And they said, I-won't-stop-you.

This must sound curious.

Well curious or not.

They thought me hysterical.

I know when someone thinks me so.

I see your fingers twist into your dress-folds.

Goodness I'm being dramatic.

The reason being that I can.

And the reason being that perhaps I must. I find this whole thing significantly funny. That's why I laugh. Not from being fine but from thinking this is funny. So never say, why-are-you-laughing? Because I'll never say, because-I'm-fine. I admit it's something. It's dramatic.

But I need first to sink into a groove. So that when I'm not in your office my chair holds my shape. As in: a shadow of myself.

No matter the fat-faced stranger squeezed into it earlier.

Listen-listen. I am trying to flatten her echo.

Often with Number Four my chair was missing. The most detrimental to my upwardness. Hard to say why. Though it seems to do with harmony. Something with identity and property. And there was a stool

instead. Or a battered loveseat from some dusty cellar.
Listen. I've walked in sobbing only to sit on floors trust
me and I've stood rather than use a dusty old loveseat.

I flew into the clutter. For good.

Well just it felt so detrimental. It feels so.

It's now a blur in my headspace.

The shopping center sends me into a fright. It sends
me flying into parked cars. Everything tries to pound
its way out. Little birds in my gut. And so on.

I try to keep both shoes planted.

Trust me how they say, bloom-where-you'replanted, or some such. I know what that means. But
listen I've uprooted and replanted. Meaning: you bloom
and rebloom. As now I'm planted right in my chair.

And you can memorize me from yours.

How I sit like this.

I talk like this.

Are you listening Number Six?

I told Number Five to talk to her others. To have
them keep my chair in its exact floor grooves. I said,
we-could-leave-them-a-note. Something like, dear-girls-
please-do-not-rearrange. Something like, please-do-
not-ever-swivel-the-chair. Meaning: if I can sit still goodness knows if I can sit still after a day of long hard
standing in tightening shoes.

Well if I can anyone can.

I told Number Three, a-note, and she laughed. I
gave a, why-are-you-laughing? She gave a, really-

you're-funny. Inappropriate I say. And I even offered
to help write the note. And I make the same offer to
you. Meaning: if you would want a note. Meaning: to
the others. Later perhaps. Meaning: I can stay later.

I found a bag in my father's car I told you. A shop-
ping bag. As my girlfriends screamed I reached inside.
There was a book. A scarf.
And the bag was there one week gone the next.
Insignificant.

My life was fine.
And then.
The slightest change trust me.
I'm just saying that any change here too would be
significant. As in: a time in Number Two's office when
a floor plant sprouted an enormous blossom of some
sort. It was hard to hold it in. What was it we decided?
Hard to say. Something with life. It sent me sobbing
screaming pulling fistfuls of hair.
Once Number Five wore a red dress. Scarring.
And Number One. I could see it clear. Meaning: I
knew what I shouldn't have known. That there was
another. Big-deal, you're thinking. You-know-there-
are-others.
Yes but her name was on the desk in plain view.
Meaning: important.
Flight.
You're thinking, jealousy.
But none of that chatter.

This is about fixing my life. This whole thing here this office. And my life is what? Memorize. Father. Mother. Two cars. One red. A garden. What else? A house. Girlfriends. And me me me I suppose. Then one day. One long hard day of standing. Well all breaks loose. That's life. The way things break loose. The way we fly out of doors fingers in our hair. The way I fly. I'm made of little birds.

Let's pretend we're girlfriends at the shopping center acting dramas. Like when shopping with girlfriends how dramatic.

Let's pretend we're flashy. We can run the staircase being knockouts. We can try on expensive dresses. Red ones.

I know what you're thinking.

But listen. I'm fine. I'm flashy in the three-way.

I know you're thinking, pretend.

But listen. I'm thinking, upwardness.

Goodness I've been through this and through this and through this. All of it infringing on the world. Meaning: my life.

As in: the day all broke.

Well I was at the shopping center that day pretending with my girlfriends in red dresses. Screaming with my friends in the three-way. Funny.

I always wondered of the bag under my father's car seat. The book the scarf.

It wasn't the first bag there one week gone the next. I wondered of them all.

Regardless.

Listen you can't stop me mid-flight.

How would you stop me?

You can't touch me.

Touching is inappropriate unless I ask. Number Three tried to hold my hand and let's just say.

Well I don't want to feel you.

Number Four and her books. She lent books. It was all I could do. As in: is this her hair? Is this a red thread? Did her lover buy her this book? It has a funny feel of something. And then the question of the lover. Old or young? Fat or thin? The rest. Trust me. Married? A father? And on and on in the man-shaped shadows.

Your fingers at your dress-folds suggest, not-important. I'm-ignoring.

Or is it, move-on. Or, go-deeper-perhaps. Deeper-inward.

Or, what-happened-next?

Well nothing much.

Number Two had this type of floor plant I told you. Listen they sprout enormous blossoms. I know these plants trust me. They grow in shopping centers. Everyone knows. With no windows and crowds and crazy echoes.

Curious.

They still grow to this big.

They were my best girlfriends.

My father called us knockouts.
He called them knockouts. Not me really.
He called me their shadow. My girlfriends'.
He called me chatterbox. His little on-and-on.
But I never chattered about the bags in his car.
Books. Scarves. Notes.

I've sunk into a groove in my chair.
Are you memorizing me? My talk?
I know you're thinking, frightful. It's funny.

What would you do if you saw me in a crowd? You see me flying from the shopping center about to scream into a fit. And there you are. And there I am. And what if I wore a red dress that day? Would you laugh at me? Would you whisper to your girlfriends? Would you say, I'll-tell-you-later-about-that-girl-in-the-ill-fitting-dress. She's-my-patient-that-girl. I'll-tell-you-why-she's-flying-into-parked-cars.

Would you ever wear a red dress because your girlfriend wears a red dress? And she looks flashy in that dress but you don't. But you thought you would look the same as your girlfriend so that when you tried the dress at the shopping center you saw your girlfriend in the three-way instead of yourself but when you got home the dress looked terrible like a binding and you wanted to throw it at your father screaming, listen-listen-listen, and instead it hangs on the back of your door reminding you that you are you.

Would you push me into the clutter knowing what you know?

I went to the shopping center. It was Saturday. My father drove us. As my girlfriends screamed I reached for the bag. It was there one week. Gone this week.

I know you're thinking, so-what. A-bag. There-were-often-bags-hidden. Scarves. Dresses.

And I never chattered. Except in my headspace.

We ran the staircase off our rockers. We looked exact in the three-way. We bought red dresses. We rode home in quiet. My girlfriend's father dropped me off at the corner. I crouched behind a parked car. I slipped the red dress over my clothing. A surprise for my mother and father. I was a knockout. Though it felt tight that way like arms squeezing my ribcage.

I could hardly walk.

My mother was in her garden in a pile of shirts. And inside in the mirror my dress looked terrible like a binding.

Do you think this will work out for us?

What I said to Number Two:
    Why-do-you-love-your-lover?
    Why-do-you-love-your-daughter?
    What-has-she-done-for-you?
    What-can-I-do-for-you?

Whose-name-is-that-on-the-desk?
Is-she-a-flashy-knockout?
Do-you-think-I-even-care?

It was me at home then. Blooming where planted.
My father was anyway not around to drive us. And I anyway had a fright besides.
Well imagine.
Numbers One through Five could never. Scarring.
It shows on the outside like something tight. Do you see it?
So this is what I told them. I'm-leaving-now. You're-no-good.
They opened their doors.
I flew down the staircases.
I chattered to myself on the streets.
You think I said, shattered. I said, chattered. Fix-me. It came back. Fix-me.

I didn't think they would let me go.
I'm speaking of One through Five not my father.
I know you're thinking, significant.
But you can't fix me Number Six.
I've hit my ceiling again.

You should memorize his red car pulling up out front. There was rain on it but it hadn't rained. You should memorize the corner of dress sticking out from the car door. I know what you're thinking. It wasn't a red dress though. It was black or blue or flowered. I know what you're thinking. It wasn't my girlfriend. It wasn't a knockout. It was some fat-faced stranger. Try to memorize this stranger.

In-a-scarf, you're thinking.

I really don't know.

With-a-book.

I don't know. I wasn't curious.

Though it would make sense.

Regardless.

It was almost dark by then.

And I've hit my ceiling.

But I'll finish the sidetrack.

He picked his shirts off the lawn. Filthy pulled from the garden. He shoved his shirts into a bag. My mother stayed put. He tried to put his coat around me. He tried to put his arm around me. I say inappropriate. And my new dress felt terrible like a binding over my clothes. Airtight. Like scars. Like arms squeezing birds from my gut.

He was on his knees.

He tried to hold my hand.

FIVE

Stay with me.

There was a time when I felt a little more and we went for walks and rides. Me and the one who gave me the kids. That was before and now is here. The yard looks quiet tonight and every night.

A tornado of fireflies spins around my chair and the point at the bottom digs out a message in the dirt. It writes, run away now! I say, they all ran away. But you never go anywhere, it says.

No that's not true. I went to different islands.

Not by yourself, it says. Never on an exclusive voyage.

I don't need an exclusive voyage.

There's a lot going on around here anyway in the yard and over there in the house. The tea kettle goes off in the cold weather and the flower garden grows in the warm. Often I sleep the whole night in the yard.

What a pretty night when the moon hits the patio. We like to be outside me and sometimes a cat from around. Squirrels watch us from a tree. The cat puts its paws up on the chair.

Flutter up under my dress, I tell the fireflies, and tell me what you see. You know I'm lopsided and getting up in years. There is rust on the trees and a flat bicycle tire stuck in the fence. The lawn chair grabs the skin on the backs of my legs.

The newspapers still land in the yard. But I canceled the delivery. Nothing works out the way it should. Cats circle the house. So do squirrels. On cool nights we all do a dance on the patio. On hot nights we sleep hard as cement.

Flutter up around me, I tell the fireflies. I'm the biggest sun and you're the dimmer stars. Take this! with my rolled up newspaper and your wings flutter up in circles like burnt charcoal. I'm the big bright sun. You're the dimmer stars. Take this!

The fireflies guide me through the yard. There is not much to see except shadows of a flat wheel and a moon glare on the car. I reach for the garden hose and shake old water out the end.

In my head is a sidewalk café. There is an Eiffel Tower too and I am fluent. Pigeons take bread crumbs from my fingers. The last of the sun beats down on my hair. A storm approaches and I open an umbrella. I notice the cracks in the sidewalk and men smoking thin cigarettes.

You do something wrong you get yelled at. The rest of the time you get ignored. Well except when you are visibly expecting. Then you get treats and you can put your feet up on the table.

There was a time before everything when we went for rides and walks. Me and the one who gave me the kids. There were days that were long and black. There were ones too that were brighter. I felt a little more at times. I felt a little less. I tried to leave the kids somewhere but how attached they could be. I had to keep them it turned out or I would have been chased. I would have been caught. I tried to leave them on the sand. I would not have minded running to another country. And they certainly could have found a better home.

The one who gave me the kids had a gravity force. Lightning bolt eyes. He wandered the beach. He was so thin he could dodge raindrops. He could stay dry in a hurricane. We went for rides in his van. We saw the whole peninsula. In the van his hand was hot on my knee. It felt as if I could be his one. Clouds parted. Trees lined the streets.

His name still escapes me.

We saw wild horses eating wet grass. Sure I would go with him to the hidden place where the trees made a circle. We ended up on the wet grass because of laziness. We ended up in the shallow water. The clams dug holes in the shape of a V and I spread my legs. We ended up in my single bed. I could hear the waves rush up and up. They fell to pieces of foam and shell not far from the window.

What a mess on my white sheets.

I watched him slink around in the shadows. He opened a box and took out my money. And then I fell asleep.

(This is how he tried to murder me in a dream. He pulled down the sun and wore it as a hat. It formed a halo of gold points around his head. He kissed me and the sun poured through my mouth. The heat pushed my skin outward and loose onto the ground. My bones gave in. He left me in a pile of ashes by his feet.)

When he left the room there was a feeling of wait come back. I am certain I said something sad. Was it not mutual? What came out was certainly unexpected. And what a remarkably short goodbye both times.

Colorful birds land in the back seat of the car where I have planted a bright flower garden. Weeds grow up out of the springs. I have planted rows of bright flowers in the back seat of the car because surely it gets hotter in the car than on the porch. I take the garden hose to the car and sing to the flowers.

Flutter up around me, I tell the fireflies. The flowers are growing look at that.

A whole year has passed. This is what I said. It took you long enough, is what I should have said. He played a penny whistle and wore no shoes. I broke the whistle into useless pieces. Look at me, I said. Nowhere else. I gave in to his gravity force. We did it on the floor with the boy screaming his head off in a cardboard box. I said the boy belonged to someone else.

(This is how he tried to murder me. He dragged me out to the sand. He pressed his hand to my mouth. He said, a girl on the sand is the first step. A girl on the sand is nothing more than a pebble that needs to be thrown. His eyes were cracked with red lines. I think now maybe he was joking. Or else he was mad. I was too tired to scream.)

I fell asleep on the sand. He carried me inside. In my head I attached myself to his legs so he could not walk. The door slammed and I cried out nothing. It would have been worse had he not touched my eyelids before leaving. I was alive though my money was gone. What a glow I had.

I am certain he feels nothing but old right now.

His name escapes me. The one who gave me the kids. His name escapes me now. Everyone said he was no good. He just walked around and went for rides. All the more reason to pursue. I think I taught him a lesson or more. Or else he would not have come back that second time.

There was a time when I was thin as a hair. I could dodge raindrops. There was a time I was wider. Everyone smirked behind my back. Most said I was too fat with that second one. Some said, you look wonderful, before they turned away smirking. I look like a planet, I cried. How could I avoid salt when it was everywhere? It was in the water. And the air.

I pushed the second one out too soon. The doctors whizzed in fast speed while I crept backward. Do you ever knock, I said. Get out of my house. I tripped over my blanket. The doctors whizzed through the room wearing miners' hats and I paused and let them get me. You got me. No there were no complications. He's the one expecting, I said. I pointed to the wall where he once stood. See look at the way his body curves. He's expecting. I thought his shadow left a print. He was expecting all puffed out like that. It was painful to look at him. He was all buckled out like that. I sensed he was carrying a girl. His face was twice its size.

I said to the wall, you big life maker you. Give *me* a few more good years! I said, I'm going to read the paper now do you mind? I put my feet up.

I said, I would know if I were expecting. It makes you feel so different. Some days a goddess and some days a kangaroo.

The doctors said no it was *me* who would be doing all the work. I said, well then knock me out. I was all buckled up. They knocked me out.

We were all together in a small house at the ocean. Once a boy and once a girl with their too soft skin and hair. Imagine how loud in the house. Sure I wanted everyone gone.

We ate crab claws and candy and the boy almost choked. His teeth never grew in right. We all kept late hours. They had terrible colds. Pink eye and rashes. I sold a watch. I took the kids to the city. I left an address. The ride to the city was hot as anything even with the windows rolled down.

We've done fine without him, I said to the kids. We're in the big city.

I also said, fireflies don't sting or bite. They just fly slow and light up yellow like that. They look as if they could bite you though. Then I bit the kids on the cheeks for a little scare and nothing felt right again. I bit her a little harder than him. I bit both of them a little harder than I had to but it was only play. Then things changed so much I wanted to bite her whole head off for being such a princess. What distance! As if the entire universe came between us. The fireflies lit up the yard.

The dog that chews the roses off the bush next door. He's your father. This is what I said. He knocked me up with a blink of his eyes.

You're driving me to the madhouse, is what I also said.

Well it could be that I drove them out eventually. Not literally of course since the car has served as a garden for quite some time. Ha. There are flower beds in the back seat.

In the shadow of the Eiffel Tower roses extend. Cigarette ashes float around my hair. Take me away boys, I say. Touch me here. You'll never know how I need it. Let's hold hands and more.

I bought crystals to make things easier. We all felt good for awhile. I carried the crystals in the pockets of my bathrobe and each one had a different kind of luck. There was luck for big money and luck for fame and luck for true love. There was luck for good health. I wanted luck for true love the most.

I dyed my hair red to be attractive.

The boy stayed in his room the girl in hers.

The crystals fit nicely everywhere. I waved them over the kids' faces until they were too big to let me.

The man who drives the bus is your father. So is the thunder and your precious sun hiding behind a storm. This is what I told the kids. Follow the yellow lines in the road to find him. Ha.

There were some things I said that made changes all around. Stay with me. Then the door slammed shut. Not once but four times. Five if you include when I locked myself in. No six. The cat.

There were other things which were not things I said but things I did. Biting the kids' cheeks. It must have scared them quite a bit. Her nightmares must have been terrible. My teeth left tooth-prints for a good twenty minutes.

What did I want? Nothing but the best for every-one. I kept an eye on them for a few years and then I said, please go. But does anything work out the way it should?

We sat in the dining room together one last time. She had brittle bones and papery skin. He had ropy veins and blood going in fast speed. When did they get so old? The tabletop had grown a black soot. Did anyone like my cooking?

The wind is going to lift our house up and carry it away, I told the kids. We're going somewhere on a cloud. The way they looked at me as if I were no influence. We're going to Oz or something.

The day the boy left for good I saw such a long shadow. I turned the garden hose on the girl to snap her out of her dream. This is as good as anything, I told her.

We've done fine without him. This is what I whis-pered to the dirty walls.

The wind shakes the leaves out of the trees. And violently. There must be a storm on the way.

The point of the tornado of fireflies says it is my turn to take a journey. I don't need to.

Now the fireflies scatter and cannot decide how to be. The trouble of making a good decision!

We once took a sea voyage to the islands. We took a bus when we got there. And a smaller boat. We saw some tropical birds. There were turtles living on all the rocks.

I turned the kids loose on a quiet beach. I set them up with two shovels and a pail. I put handmade four leaf clovers and small crystals in their pockets for good luck. Drink this sea water babies. It'll split your minds wide open. This is what I said to the kids. I walked backward. I waved. They looked at me. They were standing still. I walked backward until they were dots.

I put crystals in the flower beds to make the plants grow stronger. I found an earthworm in the dirt on the back seat. It seems it was looking for an opening.

In my head there is a path lined with shrubs. Men drink out of teacups and smoke thin cigarettes. We hold hands beneath the Eiffel Tower. Sure I will see where they want to take me. Perhaps we can wait for the storm to pass.

There was a time when I felt a little more and I took them to the city. Forget the one who gave me the kids.

There was a night I paused on the sand singing about my sweet baby doll. I have a sweet baby doll. A doll a doll a doll. All of a sudden a doll is what.

There was a night I pointed up. See that dark dot in the moon? That's your father. He's waving look at that.

Standstill

The line is long, as lines often are, no matter,
though it's tight as well, compressed, one person touching another it seems, but not really touching, just close
enough to if wanted, though no one would want it, to
touch the woman ahead, the woman behind, these
utter strangers from strange houses, effortless to touch,
not even an outstretch, yet they would flinch outright,
as, funny, no one wants to share space, a worry of
today, for instance: as on buses how it seems one
would rather stand than squeeze between strangers, a
worry, and no one wants to wait in line, another worry,
and another being that there are always lines, often
long, so no one wants to be here now, safe to say, but

one can't get caught up in negativity, for lack of a
better word, one can't let a line ruin one's morning,
for it's better to look ahead, to see toward the front of
the line, symbolic to think, to see toward the counter
waiting, to the woman behind the counter, or just to
the woman here in front, here in this standstill, close
enough to touch, and funny to think how close one
could get, but of course not to touch, to get just close
enough to share the same space, close enough to see
snags on her dress, lint, closer now to see sweat on
her neck, a wrinkle, now almost touching and close
enough to breathe her perfume, to see each hair on
her head, therefore to see each hair twitch, seeing,
therefore, that her head shakes, just a twitch and
slightly, but nevertheless a shaking, and the question
these days is always: from what, but first the answer
is: don't look, meaning: if you can't help don't look,
and who these days wants to help, as one hasn't got
the time, or, for lack of a better word, the proclivity to
help a stranger, a poor old shaking woman, though
on closer inspection, funny, she isn't even old, one
can tell from her hairstyle, haphazard, pulled back
and up, yet those loose hairs up top quiver, this from
the fact that her whole head shakes, just slightly, and
in today's world one wants to know: from what, one
always asks, one always guesses, meaning: if not from
age then from what, meaning: from an excess perhaps, of pills perhaps, or slighter than an excess, as
in: one pill too many perhaps, just enough to cause a
shaking, a slight jerking, fine and good, but the question remains: why too many pills, then the question
of: what were the pills for, meaning: were they pre-
scribed for shaking, or did they cause her to shake,
see, it gets deeper and deeper, the chicken or the egg,

the thrill of perhaps this, perhaps that, so that one places bets with oneself, see, though it could be elementary, meaning: five dollars says the twitch comes from something elementary, meaning: something slight and harmless, the air perhaps, the most elementary fact of the dirt in the air, how it's hard to inhale it these days everyone knows, this silt on the air these days you can see as a static, so that her head shakes from the air, so faintly, as faint as this line moving, so faint no one can see it it moves so barely, yet the counter is coming closer it seems, the woman behind the counter is growing, sighing, calling: next, the line tightens, and this woman in front is shaking from the air, just plain impurity, for lack of, yes, that sounds about right, impurity, a decision has been made, meaning: game over, call off all bets, from impurity, as enough already, these days, goodness, one must make up one's mind, for instance: if two boys like a girl the mother tells the girl: just make up your mind, and, you'll be an old maid, and, one boy or the other or you'll end up with neither, and, a decision please, not this touch and go, so be it, the air, but not from impurity, as the air wasn't always impure, but from the cold, a decision: the cold, that she once stood in the cold, so what, but for hours, with no coat, as elementary as that, or no shoes in the snow, thrilling, so she was locked outdoors, underdressed in the cold, which will make one shake, but look it's getting messy again, the bets are on again, as today all one does is pick pick until it bleeds, so what, a day in the snow, so what, could she still be cold and shaking from chills, or could she have gotten lastingly sick that day, well, five dollars says the shaking is from sickness, sure, she got sick, a day in the snow with no shoes, an answer less thrilling but easier on the head, so that one could ask her: what happened, and she could reply: oh it's from this illness see, it started from a cold see, from being in the cold that is, it has this long dragging name, and one could say: yes, I see, and, sorry to hear that, oh it's nothing really, it never bothers me anymore, besides, who can help if it already happened, she lived through it didn't she, meaning: here she stands here in front, so perhaps she was dragged indoors at the last possible fraction of the last possible second before she got truly ill from the cold, and now, so what, she shakes, a twitch, a nervous jerking of the head, as if something tosses about in her skull, perhaps her own questioning tossing about, how symbolic to think, shaking from one's own questions, how deep, as in: why did they drag her indoors, why was she saved, and why must she shake shake always this incessant shaking like the tick tick of a clock, a thought worsening the shaking, but lucky lady you were saved, one wants to shout this, lucky! you were brought into the warm house, years passed, here we are, and really you can barely see the shaking, it's only a result of the closeness and tightness of the line that one can see it, funny, so what, a twitch, a strange woman's torment, who really hasn't seen worse, who hasn't seen true pain and suffering in this day and age, just look around the bus sometime, it's all one can do, well then, that's that, story over, leave the stories to the storytellers and such, then one can get on with the busy events of a day, as in: the slow moving of the line, an effortless transaction with the counter woman: hello so long, then a climb onto the bus, a race through the streets amidst all those strangers with all their strange lives, the busy life of today, and the

counter woman says: next, the line advances a step,
yet still it grows at the end, so much so that its parts
are squeezed a bit tighter, compressed, and now it's
apparent from closer inspection that the twitch seems,
for lack of a word, violent, as if a larger force were at
play, if one can be slightly, for lack of a word, over-
wrought, as an unnatural force perhaps seems at play
it seems so violent, so angry, haphazard, as if a large
finger were poking one side of her head, poke poke
poke, but why not leave it, a stranger, a twitch, leave
it, but one must continue to ask these days: from what
from what, if not from age, nor the air, nor the cold, if
not from sickness of sorts, then it's a result it seems,
not a result of heredity, as in: when you reach a certain age you will get this shaking, not a result of the
bodily breakdown, as in: and it will worsen and
worsen, but a result of an outside happenstance, meaning: this happened and now this happens, a reaction,
for instance: when a perfume bottle falls from a
countertop and lands, think, well, it rolls about and
rolls and rolls until it comes to a standstill, someone
yells, for instance: pick up that bottle, or for instance:
when a girl is bad she receives a smack, the blood
rushes, the handprint remains hot on the cheek, well,
our lady here is merely still hot, she's merely still reeling from a fall, from a negative happenstance, for instance: from a prank, for instance: from a smack, or
from the obvious: her mother her sister her brother,
one's own blood causing her to fall, then shake, or
did she shake first, the chicken or the egg, here the
head spins again around and around trying to locate,
to pinpoint, to place this lady under a microscope, to
find the answer, the detail, in other words, to trap her,
as if she never felt trapped, as if she never felt walls

against her back, as if she never felt the trapped of
being trapped outdoors, as in: it's snowing and I'm
stuck out here back pressed beneath the overhang, or
the trapped of an escape from punishment, as in: turn
please back to the wall, this hurts me more than it
hurts you, and so on and so on, for instance: trapped
at a dance how the walls are the warmest place in the
room, how there were two boys to choose from for
dates, two boys from the same school and a fist-fight
in the yard over the whole damn dance, and our lady
chose none, the mother laughed: old maid, look what
you've started, just pick just pick, and give a boy to
your sister and now, and here this lady shakes her
head back back back, as if returning to this memory,
not exactly returning to the past, as one can never
return to the past, as if the past were a fixed place
somewhere on the globe imagine, as if one could visit,
begin again, well, one can't, though of course neither
can one escape, meaning: the past is both impossible
to visit yet impossible to escape, ask our lady, she has
her back to the wall which touches the past on the
other side, and the wall whispers: from what from
what, poor lady, but these days one enjoys these effortless pictures, a back to the wall, as in: the wallflower, for lack of anything better, if you will, but they
exist, wallflowers, they exist often, for there was a
dance at the school, see, our lady was there in a spring
dress, a hairstyle, and she never shook back then, she
never shook but once when she got locked out of
doors, an accident, in the cold start of spring, goodness, well, nothing but bed-rest for our lady after that,
and pills, punishment once healed, weeks later, as in:
back to the wall, her mother gave her a smack, the
blood rushed to the skin in the shape of a hand, and

the counter woman says: next next next, and, goodness, listen up strangers, no one wants to be in here
all day, stuck, trapped in this ludicrous line, this torment, for what, an elementary service, a transaction,
an effortless: hello hello how can I help you thank
you and so long, and this lady who shakes, this utter
stranger, is almost up, though who knows how long
she will take once up, just think of the way her eyes
must jiggle, the way she must see two things at once,
is that how it would be, it seems so, back and back,
yes, it seems doubled, it is doubled, dizzying, as ahead
there are two women now at the counter, behind there
are two long tight twisting lines, doubled faces stare
all around, what a rush, the proclivity to continue staring through jiggling eyes, it's all one can do to keep
busy in this ludicrous line, though it must be tiresome
to see double always, and one must ask, as one slows
down one's head: why did she not choose one boy or
the other, when her mother said: old maid, pick pick,
it must have been confusing in the head, the chicken
or the bone, well, certainly our lady went to the dance
anyway, she kept her face together, she wore a good
spring dress, an up high hairstyle, her sister's perfume,
and, sure enough, stood by the wall where it was
warmer, darker, like a wallflower, if you will, waiting,
for what, for a dance, if you will, and where were the
two boys, the ones who fought in the yard, well, somewhere, safe to say, as the counter woman chants: next
next, almost, goodness, the thrill of getting closer, one
can feel it in one's very bones, a tingling, the thrill,
and funny, thinking of the dance, viewing through
the microscope, one can see our lady had a date, yes,
there he is holding her punch in one hand her purse
in the other, an utter stranger it seems, this date to the

dance, and her sister is there, somewhere, she's off
doing her own thing, successfully, safe to say, hard to
believe she's a success, this prankster who locked our
lady out of doors in the cold start of spring after our
lady had taken a hot bath, suffice it to say our lady
shook that night, a temporary shaking, as the cold
had filled her open pores, and everyone was in a state
that night, except the sister and now, safe to say, except the mother who playfully patted the sister on the
lower back, swatted her down the stairs, playfully that
was, before turning to our lady yelling: what right had
you going out of doors, goodness, in the snow, her
brother cried, her sister the prankster, so what, most
sisters are, and what really matters is the cold ended
and everyone recovered well and good in time for the
springtime dance, end of story, a finished story, though
first our lady was delivered quite a smack the night of
the dance, a bit late, no matter, this lady still went to
the dance, a handprint glowing on her face, and she
kept her face high, though her date was too young
and fat, dirty, poor-postured, and she gave him five
dollars to go away, to take a walk, though he stood
there near, and she looked so sad, so distraught, that
at once he thought he should touch her, he should
look as a proper date, and he linked her arm, it was
so faint, so sweet, for lack of, yet she flinched, who
was he to touch her, this stranger, and she ran outdoors to break down, walked, eventually found herself home, standing beneath the overhang with
thoughts of escape, a climb onto the bus, a swift escape to some part of the globe, for good, but her
mother dragged her indoors, led her to the bath, safe
to say her date never spoke to her again, what a sad
sad shame, all one can muster in today's world, a click

of the tongue, is there anything I can do, said insincerely, but why insincerely, goodness, what would it be to touch this lady, to link arms to say: you have a friend, you have someone who understands, perhaps we can talk, and she will chant: it never really happened, what do you mean, it never happened, her personal chant: it never really happened, it never really happened, and what does that do to chant this lady, one has to know, one in a better mind-frame has to ask, it never really did, what does that do lady to chant this, nothing ever happened, right, nothing ever happened, sure, lady, your mother loved you, your brother loved you, see, one has to ease the story, to trickle it in as a storyteller would, as a friend would, your sister loved you too, and she wasn't very pretty, she never hurt you, it was a trick, her prank, all the while stroking this lady, easing the story, she never meant to punish you, this sister, dragging you, and she wasn't so pretty, she loved you most, the anger was high, but it was a trick, a ludicrous prank, she never, sure, her fingers were clenched but, the next thing you know, well, one hand tight across your mouth, the other around your waist, is that how you remember, but it never really happened, sure lady, your sister loved you, stroking all the while, easing the story as any good person would trickle it, and she wasn't so pretty deserving of two boys fist-fighting in the yard over her, but there they were fighting over her, not over you, no one fought over you, but nothing happened, sure, just your towel dropped, the perfume bottle rolled and rolled, she never had two boys, sure, there was no fist-fighting in the yard over her, that prankster, no two dates for your sister, if she wanted, easing the story for our lady, no ha ha in your

face when your mother suggested sharing, a boy for
each of you, ha ha, your mother laughed too, telling
your sister: give your sister one, calling her an old
maid, ha ha, and later your sister dragged you from
the bath, one hand over the mouth, one around the
waist, she wasn't about to share, do you remember it
this way, she dragged you to the door, pushed, the
door slammed shut, the lock clicked, and it was quiet
in the cold, dusk, the last snowfall, squirrels, the snow
sounding like tiny bells, filling the air like static, the
sky dark white and lovely as from a picture, what a
rush, the boys red-faced tangled in their fist-fight, well,
at least they stopped fighting to take a look, and no
one laughed at first, no one laughed, but the fighting
stopped, no one doubled over laughing at your undressed skin, your quick recognition, your covering
up, therefore, unable to bang on the door, hoping
your brother wouldn't open but your mother or even
your sister, your: please let me in, so quietly: please, it
never really happened, no lady, it never happened,
the thought of running, the thought of making a run
for it to the bus through the streets to a part of the
globe where no one knew you but it was too cold,
besides you were undressed, wasn't that funny, ludicrous, that there you were undressed in the cold, snow
under your bare feet, trapped against the house beneath the overhang, laughing quietly, and no one else
was laughing, no one was laughing so hard doubled
over, but, yes, they were laughing, you were all laughing, thankfully, for you see the laughing saved you,
the laughing brought your mother to the door at the
last second, though she shrieked, dragged you in by
the hair, the arms, and the room was warm and yellow, and all of those names she called of: dirty dirty

dirty all for a ludicrous date, one of your sister's boys, and your sister whispering up the stairs: tell and I'll get you, I'll get you good, and the shaking that lasted through the night, through weeks, and so on, but after a while no one laughed, except your sister, no one cared, though your mother remembered to deliver that smack on the night of the dance: what right had you, smack, the blood rushed, it hurts me more than you, and so on, keep your dress on, and your brother cried all the time, didn't he break down, you were so blue in the face that first night it gave him a scare, it felt touch and go, ask your brother, touch and go, though you could never ask him now, he doesn't speak to you now, why should he, didn't he try his hardest, can you give him some credit, he cried, can you credit him for giving a damn, can you, this younger brother with the negative posture who didn't want to dance but stood there all night slumped in front of you, looking at the older girls, and didn't he try his hardest to link arms to make you look good to make you feel a little better like you had a date, and isn't one date, any date, better than none at all, lucky lady, so what your sister had two, so what they laughed and laughed at the dance, your sister and her two dates calling you impure, the names of dirty dirty, your brother tried to help so give him some credit for giving a damn when you needed help, when you flinched outright, when you ran homeward and your mother dragged you in, saw your face so distraught, left you alone in the bath, the pills were there in the bottle on the counter, a few leftover from the illness, and no one gave a damn, it was too late, the pills didn't help but hurt, made you break down and shake, and I will try to help since pills are no help, since no one will help you, since no

one for lack of a word loves you, let me try to help
you since no one else loves you, and in today's world
one doesn't do enough, so let me try to love you, let
me stop you from shaking, as I give a damn, and I
think if I just hold your head, see, you're up now,
you're next, if I could just hold one side of that shaking head and the counter woman there if she could
just hold the other side, and if you would just let us
squeeze until you stop shaking, if you let us hold you
here tight like this, how a mother should hold a child,
how a proper girl should hold her sister, how you
never let your brother, so we're no longer strangers,
we're your own skin and blood, we're going to hold
you this way to stop that ludicrous shaking, to stop
that tossing around in your skull, to stop it stop it stop
this torment, so you no longer see double, so you get
on with your day, let us hold you here like this, let us
bring you to a standstill, let us help you in this last
fraction of the very last second, it never really, stop, it
never really, don't flinch, I beg you lady, don't flinch,
I beg you, let me touch you lady, this is the front of
the line now, and believe me lady, it gets no better.

Start

I saw houses. They were mostly big and between the houses were yards. I sought one house specific and it was biggest. Its yard was widest.

And from inside this house you could look through to the yard. I had once looked. And I could see the next house lesser in the distance.

I had once tried to see inside this next house. This lesser one. Believe me I had once strained for a look.

And here I drove in a long white dress.

A song sang out clearer as I got closer.

The heat wilted everything who wouldn't say it and I could see at last the house specific. The car hissed forward toward it.

But here I could not see the whole yard as the yard went around to the sides and back.

Lucky as the car drifted it all unfolded. I soon saw rows of chairs. The narrow aisle. The shrubs were shaped as blocks and rings. And over us all rain clouds swelled.

It would storm I predicted and hard.

The cake was enormous I could see from the car and I saw handshakes and pecks of the sort they do. Everyone wedged into crowded rows.

They shimmered in a heat haze. I could not make out faces. It was a strain as they were not near the road. Nor could I hear voices. Just the strained song coming warped through the window. Plus the car made its clamor. Good thing the road was clear. I drifted at the lowest speed hardly moving and the car clicked and hissed.

The long stemmed flowers looked as arms and how they swooped I noticed into the aisle.

My dress creased in the car.

It was turning late I saw from the march. One then another then another.

Good thing I caught his slow steps up the aisle. Though blurred from my distance. His drooped head. Then hers I knew from her red hair. I had heard she was redheaded. Her white dress hitched in the back. The flowers swayed as arms would. They leaned in curved and should have grabbed her. There in her folds of white film. Her loose netted veil. The flowers should have twined her and pulled.

It would have been best as some shouldn't wear white. You know what type. Though black is too elegant. And gray too drab. Certainly I objected to black and gray. But don't you think white wrong for her? Wrong for that type? What a waste of a dress.

Though I wore white. Floor length and long
sleeved. I could wear it fine though it was creasing
but she!

I strained to see as I drifted. Just a drive on the
road. A leisurely drive I would call it. Just should I get
caught.

And should someone say, why your white dress?

Well, church, I would answer. Though what a laugh.

I could only see the backs of heads and necks. The
chair backs blurred from my view and all the while I
crept to a standstill. Yet at an angle. I needed to
straighten my dress.

And from where I stopped one wheel on the grass
I was houses away with no straight-on view. I stood
by the car as it hissed and clicked. The song had ended.
It had sounded full swing as I first crept up. Then it
winded down to a warble. I left the car angled on the
roadside and walked.

You're thinking, no! But you better believe. I started
walking.

The ground was soft enough to pull me in. The
gardener had over-watered. Who wouldn't say it? And
with rain coming a waste and a mess.

I tiptoed from bush to tree on the toes of my high
heels. My shoes were far quieter than the hiss of the
car. And no one was looking my way. They had all
eyes on the two.

March up there, was my one thought.

And, we are gathered here today.

And, speak now or forever.

I found a safe place in the block shaped shrubs.
The yard smelled of summer. So many gifts on that
table! Goodness knows I could have used them. And
that enormous cake. And a house or two.

I could barely hear how they uttered with the priest. Their back and forth back and forth. We all waited with ears to the air. There would be an ending soon a good one I hoped.

She was a flimsy thing. I saw I had more curve more fill. Had I changed any? A whole year had flown.

I saw I had more charm more class. Even flustered in the shrubbery. Even with darker hair and eyes with a scar denting one leg. No matter though in floor length. Though it dirtied at the hem. So sorry to the worms who saw. The gardener did some job watering. He would hear it later I predicted. Worms were popping up everywhere. And here I tried to keep myself clean in white. She was not one to wear it but hat to shoe I was white and pure. The straight and narrow. Except my skin off white and drab. Some would say. And my dark hair dark eyes. And of course my dirty shoes digging pits in the yard.

Not much camouflaged all my white in the dark shrubs. Good thing I was shadowed. No one would see me crouching. The house cast its wide shadow and I crouched in darkness and thought. That she should have worn red is what I thought. No offense though. But scarlet. But the hottest shade to match her hair. To match the day.

How his parents might have laughed once. Meaning a year before at dinner. A scarlet dress on a day as this. Ha ha they would have laughed at what that meant. And why not velvet? They would have thrown back their heads. All of us seated at the dining room table. It seemed just recently we sat. I did not have the nerve to speak up at the table. He squeezed my hand underneath and I was his I knew. It seemed so recently.

Well a whole year had flown.

Well it seemed just days.

And it seemed forever as well. Meaning stuck in the mud from that point and always. And this would always be the world. And this would always be the view.

And looking up I saw the dining room window. How odd to stand in the yard seeing all those house windows. To know that upper one was the dining room. That lower one his bedroom.

Start with the sky. The dark clouds. I predicted more handshakes more peck pecks and insects sounded in my head. The clouds could have burst at some point. I predicted foul weather. We would all run for cover.

And yet there they sat in such frilly dresses and summer suits. Crowded into tight rows all chair legs deep pitting the yard. Gleaming on the joyous day.

We would drown in mud if the rain ever started.

I could have left at any time.

I thought to march up there and take her place.

Some pointed flashbulbs this way and that.

I ducked. I was not part of the joyousness. I was minding myself in the shrubs.

And I could not leave. Partly as I was held in mud. I was thinking hard. I was thinking of a long long time. Partly for other reasons.

I counted the gifts. I certainly could have used them all. No matter what was inside and was that the dining room table holding the gifts? The good wooden table dragged out to the wet grass?

Everything felt out of place.

Trust me I had sat at the table. And as I ate that night I had looked through the window hearing of the yard upkeep. They loved to tell it and there was the gardener digging down there in the green. A shovel and bucket. See that is funny. Just that it was startling to see the table where the bucket had stood a year before. Where the gardener had shoveled dirt. And here I was in the block shaped shrubs. And there were his parents in row one. He on a platform. And this redhead in white. Where was the gardener I wondered. Perhaps in the dining room looking down. Ha ha his parents would have laughed at that too. The gardener in the dining room.

They asked of my people at dinner.

I had not meant to spill my drink. We make mistakes.

For instance I should have kept driving. What a mistake crouched behind the shrubs. Crouched behind the latecomers in their last row.

As if I never. As if we never he and I but we had! And there was no time for crying. All those swooping flowers. The darkening sky. This was to be a wonderful day and the crowd teared and dabbed. You better believe they were moved.

And we tried to ignore the priest. The big question. I dabbed on my white sleeve.

Anyone?

Any takers?

Their hands were clasped I saw this. Though loosely. She seemed so flimsy. My fingernails would have dug half moon imprints had it been my hand in his. And his would have squeezed mine as it did under the table.

I thought, what if he turned and saw my hair twined with leaves? I would pop out and wave. I would run to her place.

I thought, what if I stood amongst the gifts? I would lean on the cake. I would say, once ago we sat at this table. His parents handed foods. And I was his then. And his parents asked such strange questions of my place. And I was his one. I have a scar to prove it.

And from the dining room table I had looked through the window. I wanted to see inside the next house but I saw the yard spread for a long way and the gardener shoveling dirt into a bucket and the next house very far away.

They asked of my people.

And as I looked down to the gardener he looked up to me.

Some people are dirty in dirty clothes.

And I had spilled on the good table. A very good table so they said.

A mistake.

Start with the gifts piled high. I was close enough to touch the ribbons. To peel each shred of wrap from each package. To expose each showy gift. Oh thank you and you! A chair from the friends. A shovel from the gardener. A clean white dress from the family. And a brand new car and a lovely house. And another house! And another!

And had I said, give them back! Had I said, smash them! Smash the cake under your shoes! Cut the heads off the flowers! I dared him inward. Strip from that suit and break down the platform!

Then we could have run. We could have driven away. The car was there one wheel on the grass three on the road. The same road where I had once walked for dinner. And I wore a clean white dress that night and held a gift for his parents. And foods were handed around and around then not. I had spilled. What a waste of a drink and the glass had broken. His poor mother up like a jumping jack cleaning the spill. Then she pecked the air by my face and showed me the front door. I stood in the dark and the rain fell in buckets. Anyone would have said it and I could not run in the rain so I climbed through his bedroom window you better believe it.

And would you believe this is what I thought in the shrubs? That he lifted me through the window and we fell to the wet floor?

Start with nice thoughts.

I hardly knew him up there blocking the priest.

I could see the window I had crawled through and it was closed.

Well I knew how to open it. Just a small push. I could have showed the crowd. Just a small push then more then more.

What else could we have shown?

The good table legs sank in the mud. The gardener should have lost his job.

Once his parents commented on the troublesome upkeep. That their gardener was the best and they talked and talked and I was very poised and drifting that night at the table looking through the window until the gardener waved up and what a jolt. I spilled my drink. And there was no cake after and they smirked at my gift and showed me the front door.

And there was his mother in row one. Just a speck from where I was. There she was. Hello! His speck of a father too. All of them so dear and brittle. So easily jangled.

Well I knew how to keep quiet. Not a leaf rustled. I barely breathed and the sky turned darker. We would have to run for cover. I sought a doorway a shade tree. I sought a quick run to the back door. Or I could have slipped through the window as I did that night.

When the rain fell in buckets I had ducked right through. And I had wet hair and a wet dress and shoes. And I had to peel it away as we fell to the wet floor.

Start with the drive. I should have kept driving. That awful song. The march was it? It was earsplitting. Warped. A wind had picked up during the song and the warble. It sounded awful. I should have kept driving onward and onward. I should have driven until night and thrown out the dress. But I could not as the flowers looked so lovely and she as well and he. And I wanted to watch to see the end. To see if the flowers would grab her. If they would tangle her up to their worm-bitten roots. Well then. My thoughts were clear. I would have marched up to her place white dressed in stained shoes. Standing at the aisle top waiting. Hello! He would have turned and seen me and dropped to his knees. Believe me he had regret. He had sorrowful thoughts. When he held my hand he meant it. When my drink spilled he thought it funny. When I handed the gift he was impressed. When I whispered in the room. Well you better believe it. And we whispered even when there were footsteps in the hallway. Even when there were more than those footsteps and downpour. We ended under the blankets and the small sounds I uttered. Surprising. I uttered. Then uttered. Then screamed.

Though I never meant to. A mistake.

I hadn't expected such a jolt.

His father his poor brittle mother swatting me out from the house like an insect. Some people, they said. Some people! and out I went through the back door.

And I had hardly a stitch on and no shoes when I stumbled to the wet yard onto the shovel.

The scar still twines my leg as proof.

We could have our own house, I wrote him the next day and the next and so on. Or more, I wrote and wrote. Our own houses. To think it. Our houses and houses and we could sit in the yards. And we could let the grass grow high and the flowers wild and we could make any sounds any screams. And no gardener to care so about the upkeep. No mothers. No fathers.

And I meant for the very longest time. I meant always. With only each other as scenery. Only each other as sounds.

I expect they shredded my notes. Then they found this new one this redhead whose veil whipped around. Poor thing.

My thoughts were cluttered.

Then a thunderclap sounded.

I thought, run! That she should have. Run! Before the sky opens up and destroys your white dress! Mine was so dirty around the hem.

I would go for cover at the count of ten. We were exposed out there. I was exposed even crouched behind the shrubs and I counted. One.

Though the question asked of us.

Two. Three.

Well I thought we should run for cover and think it over. But the end was beginning. There was little time left. A thunderclap and again and everyone waited.

I thought hard and the question still hovered.

You better believe we had something. Once. His parents were dear. I would have loved them as mine. They could have changed me. Cleaned me.

I counted four.

He was smart to stay put. I had so little and she had red hair. And they had this whole wonderful yard and a gardener.

Though what a gardener with everything sinking. All chairs all heels. The good wooden table. Was he smirking in shrubbery watching everything sink?

Who were his people I wondered.

And the question hovering about and I counted five then six.

Anyone?

Any takers?

And they on the platform stood stiff. Hands loosely clasped. Ears to the air.

I thought to pop up. Out like a jumping jack. To plunge a finger into the enormous cake. To pluck a gift from the table and run. But I reached into the soft mud and it smelled of summer. I rubbed some on my dress front. On the sleeves. The song would soon start up. The dark clouds had taken over fully. The crowd had stopped dabbing. The flowers looked exhausted wilting and drooped. I rubbed mud on my neck and the shrubbery rustled. I rubbed over my scar and up my legs. And perhaps she in her white film would have liked to. I rubbed mud in my hair and it felt as rain and perhaps poor thing with the veil flapping down she would have liked to have joined me. We could have been jumping jacks in the block shaped shrubs. And I counted seven eight and she could have been like me. And I got to nine. A mess like some people. They were turned and staring.

Just like some.

Start with speak now or forever hold it.

I saw myself to the car at ten.

But first from the shrubs as the sky opened up I did object.

Trees

We had just sat to eat. A bit late for dinner but cooking took time. Steaming plates of bacon and bread and weren't we lucky? We were and with all the time ever it seemed and so we sat. The cleaning could wait. Oven pans heaped and the walls seemed streaked with dark. Was it dirt or paint? Regardless there was bacon piled high and bread.

How common that it went awry. My fork about to pierce and there it was slipped under the salt shaker. The note of codes to be deciphered. I took it to the stove. I lit the burner the boy watching waiting. I said, eat!

She went in for word tricks. To write, under a tree, could have meant in the park. It could have meant mountains. And she wrote, trees trees. There were trees drawn too. Trees down the side and up top. She wrote, off I go!

More hateful words meant one thing only. Not eating but school. That she wanted out.

I took it as a runaway note for it noted a bus. Always tricking she coded it good and then to hide it under the salt shaker our good dinner ruined. Well how very her to do just that. How her to disrupt. I had set three places too. The boy took his. I mine. I had set three in hopes of her joining but how her to leave a note and run. To ruin dinner.

She had quit all good food. All to look good but I saw frail. All for us to look. The ones in school said, skeleton! They stood at the bus stop just up the street. We could hear and skeleton yes she looked it.

It was a phase like sucking a finger.

I thought of force-feeding. Imagine the boy stretched wide her mouth. Then I poured in heavy cream and hissing fried eggs until she turned pillowy and slow.

But no luck. Her mouth always clamped. Her ribs poked jagged through a coat. Besides I thought it best to let her do hers. Best to ignore. I had an agenda of cooking. There was the cleaning and the boy. Goodness to look after every scrape and scratch on their four knees. Well I was planning a reentry into the workforce.

Should I have swung wide the door? Should I have bagged her fatty meat and cake? Heavy cream? Off you go! A wide swing into the cold. Go out there into the wide world but goodness take a coat. Just to teach her. Just to widen her. If she wanted out then out. Take a heavy dinner.

I wanted mine. It was late.

How plain for her to disrupt and I had a sink of dirty dishes. I had oven pans to scrub.

They were getting older.

She went to what trees? I took it to mean to the park where we once walked. There was a circle of trees. I told the boy to stay seated. Eat.

First I thought to ignore her. What a chance for her to widen. Out in the world. The boy said, go!

I trudged coatless through the dark my boots crunching. A layer of ice coated snow and wet. At times the wind held me stuck. I peered through the park's gate to frozen stuck trees. To the swing sets. We once went to the park we three. In spring. They played. Had the boy forgotten? There was a way to strap in on the swing set. How could she have forgotten strapping in? Goodness how it stuck with me. I reminded them too. How they went higher and higher calling me out.

No one sat even in the park that night with the wind hissing through hedges.

I could have hurried home to the sink of fatty pans. I could have thought it a phase. That surely she would return. I could have searched more through the park. But I was ice and she had noted a bus.

Every night I waited with an ear to the radio. And the boy slammed his door and hard. I waited for her voice every night. It came through cloudy then clear.

The first time it startled. I had gone in for soothing music. A switch and there was music then static then she came in faint. Low and clear I heard her voice. Faintly first then the raspy outcry of a crow that was clearly her. I pressed up an ear.

First a cloudy swarm then clearer. The wavering outcry I knew as hers.

A wave had carried her.

It sounded as though she were inside the radio. Certainly I did not believe her inside. Standing. Imagine! With her thin buttoned up coat. Absurd even. But it sounded that clear and good.

The boy said there was nothing in the radio but radio workings.

Yes I know, I told him and shook him. The waves and signals send her through.

He argued on the side of it being absurd.

But we do not understand the workings of such! She had been gone for weeks. He never knew enough to teach me. I knew more despite his smarts. For one anyway who was older? Certainly I had life wisdom. I had the ear pressed tight.

He said, if she could come through. If though. Then how in the good world could she hear me? How in the world? Questions which did not warrant an answer. School was telling him a thing or two. He said, how though? Absurd questions answered with a door slammed.

My boots slowed. It could not have been colder with the wind just whipping. It could not have stung more through such a thin shirt. I thought to find a stray coat in the bus station but mostly everyone had gone. Everyone had taken their coats and gloves. The wind had snarled my hair. What a thin shirt I chose to wear barely buttoned. I warmed by a wall and knew better than to stay long. The workers gave dirty looks. I was a sight coatless with wind-snarled hair and they made it quite clear clutching tight their mops. They gawked.

Her note had words on school and hateful words she noted. And she was fading fast. Those in school gave dirty looks with the boy as witness. She wanted stares. I saw too. The way they looked for no good reason. For example thinness. For example a sour face. Well do not look to blame me. I had the skillet full.

The catch was she wanted out of school. Out of the question! I could have schooled her sure with good books and smarts but she just wanted sleep.

Out of school and she said she would have cake. She would sit to a plate of good meat.

I said, eat cake and school will be fine. Eat meat.

I said she was just a regular target. It would blow over. Just eat.

I said, we have all been there at one point and another.

Then her note.

I said, no harm in a school yard.

The boy said, the bus stop. The backyard. The park.

I wanted no part. The workforce awaited.

The boy said, the street. The store. The playground. The backyard. The park. The park. The park!

He was asking for a shaking.

Besides I could not help her nor could the boy. He was in a grade higher and could not stoop to give a look and I was far too old to stoop. Besides she was gone for now. Problem one to get her home. Two to force-feed.

If only we could walk through the park. We three. There was no good reason. I told them they could not have fit in the swings.

She came through my ear pressed up tight. First static hissing and sputtering the sound of a coop clamor. Then her outcry. I would have known it anywhere through the sputtering. It settled into a caw.

Through cupped hands I said, I can hear you.

There was a way to hold the outcry tight with the antenna toward the door pointed.

Through cupped hands I said, where are you?

She said, with a cat.

Not just an outcry but real words came through. That with a cat.

I could give the cat a bowl of cream. She could sit at the table and watch the cat. We could have a regular dinner.

With the radio turned up high the outcry came in more clearly though so did the static come in and the boy slammed his door. Turned down more would have made her too faint was my argument. It hurt his head was his.

I often ran washroom water with the radio on full. I was trying to smother the static. The boy thought it foolish to run the radio and sink. Meaning electrocution. Impossible the way I kept the two apart but he had a good head. He would enter the workforce.

Though what a quandary with slamming doors for signals. The washroom wall tiles could not stay glued. Doorknobs loosened in my hands.

Girl. Thin. She is very quick. She is quick as a bird. She is very thin. I mean transparent by this thinness and quick. And too with a coat. With boots too and a purse. And she must be hungry and dragging her boots. She has not yet eaten for the night. She must be cold and dragging. Her fingers numb and I need her home. My fingers too have turned blue. I have walked all this way from home. I have forgotten my gloves and coat. There is dinner waiting. Bacon and bread. I have forgotten a comb. Her brother is waiting at the table. He has saved her a good portion of bacon. There will be cake. First we must find her. Her bones have surely snapped. The cold has frozen and cracked her hair. We must find her and drag her and one worker pointed and it was her outside waiting. It was her slumped waiting in a thin coat.

I called out and she turned startled and scuttled across the ice.

Her shadow seemed from a slim tree but the way it wavered as she scuttled. It was certainly her.

She ran and the cold held me. What a thin shirt I chose for that night as if the sun shone.

My boots crunched hard in the ice. She must have heard the crunching for she quickened. She went faster slipping and I said, let me drag you!

My boots slowed and pushed through the crust of ice.

First I was chasing her but she was quicker in the circle so imagine how the chase turned and she was the one chasing.

She threw ice and kept me on my knees. I had a mouth of ice and frozen shut eyes.

I thought how remarkable it turned when I was the first one chasing.

I tried, how about a walk in the park doll? We can make snow angels. How about some cake?

We were so close to the park where we used to walk. There would be some softer snow. Perhaps by a patch of hedges. I knew the place.

A bus turned its lights on us.

How about a snow angel in the softer snow? A truce. An angel in the snow just you and me. There was a round of softer snow near some hedges.

She threw ice throwing harder to keep me low and down. It cut.

A push on the swing set. We could try. Cake after dinner.

I crawled then stood. I staggered in the middle of the crumbling station and workers gawked and a bus came on. What a thin shirt I wore as if the sun poured straight through the iced windows of our dark house. There was the park where we once walked and its trees.

A push on the swings! But she was falling. Goodness she was falling low and hard. She was slipping low my knees so wet and cut I thought they would shatter. A bus was coming through. I said, let's do angels! But she was falling low. Goodness she was low in front of the bus and it felt fine to hear her cry out.

She could have frozen is all I cared. I was cut and spinning mad. The bus could have pressed her is what I felt.

One last look. She was sprawled.
A worker came and lifted her. She walked fine.
I ran home straight.

I thought it odd to walk through the door empty-handed. The boy was sleeping good.

I thought, when was it we swung in the park? When I strapped them in tight and they called me out? They said, higher higher, and the trees came closer. Then what?

Then we walked home for dinner.

I cleaned under my nails with a pin. What a night and I dug dirt rooted deep in my knees.

I slept in and out. I waked and cleaned with a pin harder until blood crept around the corners. I slept in and waked.

The sky thought to lighten. What a morning it was turning.

I cleaned again digging until the blood made a fast stream sound.

The sun crept in and I circled and scraped. I dug and crept through the hallway.

Her bed was empty. The sink was cluttered with fatty pans. The note on the table and knocked over salt. Eggshells on the trashpile.

I took a coat this time. I had learned a heavy coat. I walked to where the ice softened in bright sun and no sign of her spread. No sign of a bus. She had not slipped under a tire. I saw her upright. She had not frozen underground. The bus had not spun to its side. Had she gotten on the bus? It turns out a lighter coat would have been fine. The bus had not pressed her. She was walking fine. I knew she was teasing not being anywhere. She was putting out her codes. I said, everyone find this one. I called her out through my hands.

On the radio she said, I want to come home, it sounded.

I would fry bacon and her cat could stand close.

Perhaps it was a country cat she got on a trip. That she had taken a trip to a place where she found a cat. It seemed a country cat I knew from the thick fur I imagined.

I could have gotten her home with clues. For instance, where was she hiding?

She was asking for her brother. He was the one since it was me she wanted to cut and murder.

I lied, but I am willing to take you from school!

Still she wanted the boy.

I lied, I am willing to feed you fruit and water.

Still the boy and I said, your brother calls this absurd. You are absurd see. You are all. Meaning all of you.

All I wanted you know was me.

I did not mean it.

Then she let out static and hard. It was static hissing all night hard into my head.

I thought when she came through the door we would take her and fix her. The boy said, if though.

I thought she would step off a bus. We could go to the park. We could jump in soft snow. I sat every day in the station. My on and on question of has anyone seen her. The ones got off the buses every day and walked around as if to avoid. I followed their heels. I said every day the same question and the sky got darker blue then black and that was every night despite the weather. That was every night it got darker and blacker and I trudged home.

I thought perhaps she had coded her room and I searched her dresser. Through each sock and shirt. She never thought to fold.

I searched through her closet. Under her bed where papers piled. There was dust.

The wind shook the room. The room felt cold and I thought how she slept. I thought with the wind seeping in through a crack. The window seemed it would fold and burst.

I threw her blankets against the window. To seal up the crack. So the air would not seep.

I had poor aim. Some bottles shattered.

The boy said a question.

Get out of here!

I threw the books. They seemed full of mold. About to rot. I threw the pillows. They seemed rotted. Overfilled and crumbling and I tore them to pieces. The boy in the doorway. Go away! It must have thrilled him to see my face scarlet. I screamed, get out! And he ran my face scarlet. Oh it must have given him his life thrill. Get lost, I screamed after he had. Never had

he seen this face so red hot. I slammed shut the door.
I broke through the window. A bottle straight through
and the books too. And the pieces of pillows. The
rotten foam. The rest. Her things. Her nothing things.
They flew.

The boy and I sat for cake. A treat and weren't we
smart to think of it? We deserved something sweet
and good and we told the truth. To each other we felt
to.

The table needed cleaning. I had really put things
on a downhill. Her room was quite upended. There
would be time to clean after cake.

I would take a sponge to the walls. They seemed
streaked. Or was it the light?

The boy told she was getting cornered. Too late he
told.

He told how they trapped her.

She was a regular target.

They had poked her.

The boy was such a good boy once and once he
would have told sooner. Once he would have told
before she was out the door. I thought it was only
dirty looks.

I thought to clean the table. The sponge needed
soaking. We could wait for cake. We needed to clean
the littered lawn.

They pulled her through mud. They pulled by her
hair.

Did I know this? Had she told me? I thought it was
dirty scowls.

We would need more than an afternoon to clean
the lawn. The window needed mending. How had I

forgotten the window and cold air was blowing through. Cold air always found cracks and seeped.

She was swung by the hair. For their thrill.

I thought it was dirty words. We can take words. All words are dirty. All words are dirty out of dirty mouths. Skeleton skeleton! Even we have dirty mouths letting in our cake.

They pulled her.

Her hair. It was a stringy mess. They pulled her through streets and the streets needed cleaning. All the streets were dirty rotted. The bus stop too where she was pulled. The dirty bus stop with the dirty school bus.

The table needed upending. The whole house needed a good shaking. We had dust. And smudges. Streaks. He used to be such a good one and to think we had cake. It was so sweet and there was more on the counter.

To think I threw ice back just once. I told the boy. I threw back.

Had the boy told his sooner meaning weeks sooner I would not have thrown. I was one to give a break. I would have let her pummel me until I was cut and murdered.

To think I broke through the crust with a bare hand. I grabbed a good wet slab. There was no time to reconsider. I aimed low and I wanted to get her. Imagine me wanting to cut her and how the ice cut my hand.

The bus skidded and screeched to a spin.

To think how I wanted to cut her and she had been pulled through mud. She had been pulled through streets.

To think I thought we would take her and fix her. I would give schooling in the house. I would say, I thought they were teasing. I will teach you at home doll. You can starve so long as you are home doll. I will feed you water and grapefruit.

And to think I threw ice and she ducked and slipped in front of the bus. Meaning I missed. The ice shattered far out. At least that. I ran home.

And she was upright walking. I made certain.

And to think we could have instead swung hard in the park.

There was a way to shake the radio to make her voice strong and clear. To shake the radio a few times up and against the wall even and the voice came in much more even with the volume down to please the boy. There was the risk of breaking the radio to get the voice more clear though the more I shook the clearer and I shook it and shook it until the plug ripped from the wall and the antenna bent and radio pieces spun across the room my face red hot.

I told this truth. That a house without her was a different house. And I told a lie. Not to worry.

There was a way to strap them into the swings and how happy they were when they flew higher then higher. They called me out and how it stuck with me. I pushed them higher. And she did not want to get unstrapped. She wanted to stay moving after the boy came down. She wanted to flip over the top bar. This being every night until the sky got darker blue then black.

By the trees she must have meant the countryside. That she went to the countryside on the bus and stayed. I figured a way to crack the code. Trees trees! A thick-furred cat. She had climbed on the bus. She had climbed on the bus for surely we would have heard had she been under. Surely it would have made the paper. There would have been sirens. Anyway I saw her standing. Walking. She got on and took a country ride. A tree-lined country journey.

I told this truth. That I was often all I wanted.

We left the doors open. The wind flew through. First through her broken window. It brought the cold inside. Into the kitchen. Then an ice storm came with a gusting wind. It came flying through and shook the walls. Then the sun poured itself. And the dust showed clearly dancing. Then more ice and wet. Cold. Then the moon. And it got quiet.

There was dinner cooked. We were ready to eat. The cleaning could wait.

We sat at the table.

Vulgar

Feel for the page held with a leaf. Stare him straight.

Have him sign in the space on the page held with a leaf so he will say, what a leaf you saved. A single leaf just for him for just that page. Show the green veins. The worm hole.

He prefers his girls slight.

Eating chances a hard stare at the middle. Eating turns to cramming like a beast.

Cramming turns to dull yellow shame.

Keep the middle empty and inward behind a dark dress a slimming coat. Certain tilts of the head make a handsome hollow around the eyes and he perhaps will see how slight.

Stare him sweetly and straight. Feel how he can be fire.

The stove will not work. For seconds it hisses and sparks. It has not worked since the fall and the landlord must be reminded. The landlord so slouched in her loose skin unwilling to budge.

The landlord warm and fat in her brick house.

A working stove would warm the room.

No one wants to be out on a night as cold as this. It gets dark early the trees coated in thick ice. No one wants to chance it in the cold. Not the landlord who waits always good and long so fat and spread crammed into her warm chair. Nor your author out and about having a drink. Nor the cat the way it looks to burrow in folded clothes. Chase it before it sprawls and sheds and ruins the night.

No one wants to chance it but your author will make it out. Chances are the landlord will not.

Run hot sink water over loose tea. The water must run until hot.

It must be the landlord forgets dwellers of single rooms. A working stove would make the room warm. The landlord it must be knows this and forgets. She should have fixed the stove by now but think instead of the night ahead. The warm hall and handsome crowd.

Hold the book open with the cup and saucer to the page held with the leaf and think of the night as the tub fills.

To offer a pen would chance it. Trust he owns pen sets being an author worthy of presents.

Have him sign in the blank space above the page that gives thoughts of him drinking hard with a sharp sliver of moon outside the curtain. A clean page in the typewriter. A slight girl waiting by the bed who sheds his robe.

Feel certain he is not looking at her hollows.

The typewriter clacks and see how the girl disappears and in her place another.

The window is jammed open and cold air pushes and a call should be put in to the landlord. The night will drop cold enough to snap branches and wires.

Put in a call to the landlord. Tell her the bathroom is a room and she perhaps will have a laugh at your expense. A dweller in *two* ice cold rooms and tomorrow would be the time to have her over. There is no time tonight with the hall about to open and your author out and close and tossing down drinks.

Have him sign on the blank page in back and draw together. Make a house and have him draw the sun. A winding path with trees. Both names interlocked.

Conceal the common hard-worked skin. Chasing mice with a broom. Wrestling the cat on the floor like

a beast. What a result on the hands! Wear gloves inside no matter how warm and stare straight through.
Provoke an introduction gloved hand first.

The tea turned cold and if he were to come over
later for a night and slip off the gloves and want hot
tea then what?

The leaf blew through the open window and landed
on the table clutter during fall. If he asks to keep it
write a sweet note across the veins. His name and the
date. Say, I held on to this leaf for you for this page.
What a leaf you saved still fresh and new!

He plays the field everyone can agree and if he
were to come over later and slip off the gloves hurry
and shut the lights so he can feel how soft.

The cat leaves mice on the table. Always there are
many curled mice. When the landlord comes to fix
the stove tell her mice scurry through the jammed open
window. The cat raced through once through the window and has stayed a good long time. The landlord
has certainly waited good and long. It gets longer and
later and colder.
Undress while the bath fills hot.

The dollars spent on the book could have bought
fresh groceries. What a slim and handsome hardback

flat on the table. Look how the cup and saucer indent the page held with a leaf.

The book was costly but do not think twice. Groceries affect the middle.

The cat races across the table. Quick the teacup.

If he comes over later for a night and wants tea hot simply shut off the lights and run the water a good time until steam. Feel for the heat while he sits in the dark.

Once everyone has come together it feels warm in the hall until a vulgar girl arrives late breathless and wet-haired pulling in the cold night. Scarves will stir and settle on the chair backs.

Walking in late slices through the middle. Every head turns.

Walking in early assures the center chair in front. Squeeze between lesser fans. Sit still and pay close attention though how easy to look the other way with a handsome crowd like that. With a bright dot of moon out the door and up.

The teacup wants to topple it seems the way it tilts. One quick race of the cat and certainly the teacup will topple and look how it indents the page. The saucer would certainly catch most of the tea. It would be a good idea to take the tea into the bath. To sink almost too low and feel how warm. Hear how the bath fills up.

Do not leave the room while he reads. Nothing is important not even fresh cold air. Not even a fresh coat of lipstick. Certainly not a cigarette.

Vulgar girls who leave halfway make an author pause.

His is a rare talent the one in a million. How hot it gets and the coats want to drop off the chair backs. Every head turns to watch the vulgar girl who races head down into the fresh cold air where other vulgar girls smoke.

The joke is on them. *Did I say something to offend you? Was it my writing?* No never your writing which has a surprise at every turn! Stay in the room. Let's just get through it. The folding chairs curve awful and everyone wants dinner but let's just listen to the words together for once.

Sit on the edge of the tub and watch what the water does as it fills. It spirals see. It calms. And feel the steam opening the face closing the eyes filling the pores. An upset in the other room requires a leap but stay put. Keep the feet and legs in the warm water and sink. See the reflection in the whirlpool going deep down. See how a slight girl appears in his robe. The typewriter clacks and she comes closer trying to warm her hands.

It would be vulgar to whisper.

The upsetting crash was just the spill of water filling up and over and see how it circles like that. The legs melt down into the water. Let them and the cat races past.

It would be a rare wonder to catch him stumbling on a line. He said cats and meant eats but what a quick cover up. To tell him would chance it.

Stare him sweetly. What a handsome suit in dark slimming colors.

Have him write a special note.

Stare straight through his cold clear eyes and do not avert. See his skull and the wall behind him. Wires tangle in the wall. Mice scurry toward an opening while he holds the gloved hand while he signs and then have him write a note.

Some write, to a beautiful girl. Do not let a line of handsome fans discourage. They crowd and shove so hold tight.

Show the note to the landlord. Say, look it is a note to me. He wrote it special to me. Oh yes I know him some.

See the reflection in the whirlpool how a slight girl hovers vulgar while he works hard. She draws in his air by hovering closer still. She should not chance it. Once she feels warm by his fireplace he sends her out into the cold. Who has the time to focus on a single girl? It is hard enough to focus on the cat crying from the upset but stay put.

Do not attempt petty conversation about pleasantries. Tell him that each page contains a quite unusual twist but telling too much will chance it. Though his head could swell with pride he could look down at the middle. Really. Who are you even so false and slight? Who even in a dark slimming dress and be careful not to wrinkle in the folding chair.

Say, what a reading! What a wonderful reading!

Have him over later for a night.

Have a good long laugh when the gloves come off. It is too dark for him to notice the scratches and the table clutter. Laugh when there is no good hot tea to serve. Feel for the steam and whistle for the kettle. It certainly is a funny world. When cold air pushes mice through the jammed window. No stove to warm but he is a fireplace and there is warm water. Always there is warm water plenty enough to give. It certainly is a funny world so throw the head back and make it wonderful.

The bathwater fills higher and over. Higher and over the edge.

There is no time to bathe now anyway undressed legs dripping wet. There is no time with the book spread out on the cluttered table held open under a saucer and tea.

Dry the legs and feet and get dressed.

But there is no time to get dressed the book drowning in tea in the table clutter under sopping towels. The cup seemed sure to topple.

Turn off the bath water and toss towels on the floor.

Certainly the pen will not work on the damp page. Not even a pen from a pen set. It would bleed in the wrong way and tear the page. Certainly he cannot be handed a sopping wet page.

The page must dry. Do not slip on the wet floor. Swat the cat with the broom. Take it by the scruff and give it a good toss into the icy trees. Do not let it back until it feels shame and the tail is frozen stiff.

Have a quick drink to your rare and wonderful author. To him the most rare and wonderful. Have another one to him and another until the heat rushes through and sit and think how slight girls have lined up and how nice to see the line curves wavy out the door into the cold. Every girl wants a special note.

The page will never dry the book drowning on the table under a saucer and sopping towels. The pages stained and soon to curl.

Take the space at the end of the line under the frozen trees and wait. By the time you reach the front the page will be dry and he will be old and bent and slight when you look inside his cold clear eyes to the wall behind him.

But no. There he is fresh and new.

Say, scratch your name in the space with a pen set pen.

If he slowly looks up keep the eyes in place and stare him straight. Get his name on the page and be fine and go home to dinner.

Or ask for a special note something he perhaps is feeling right then and there. He could make it out to his dear sweet friend.

Say, the book will get its own special stand to sit higher than the lesser books.

And if he were to name the cat what would he say for a name? Name the cat whatever he says. What would he name?

Or say, it is just a book nothing else. Say, if you want to write it I am just a dear sweet fan.

Hold the book down on the table.

Say, what would you name the cat?

Feel for the wet page held with bits of leaf crumbled under tea. Wink and say, so write and let me get home to dinner. Let him see your hollows.

He could look slowly up.

Hold the middle inward.

He could turn toward you.

Hold it in and show your hollows.

A name for the cat, he could sneer.

He looks about to laugh.

Oh it seems as if you chanced it.

You asked a vulgar question.

Water warms the floor and he is going to have a laugh. The handsome crowd closes in to hear. He has in fact turned his head to have a laugh and really! Who are you even? Sweep the shattered tea cup up from under the table. When he looks down at the middle hold it. Hold it in and see there is his pen. A pen set pen on the table clutter. Hold it and see how heavy. How costly. Unscrew the cap. Certainly it was costly. Hurry in your pocket and run to the door. The cat cries now good and rigid and full of shame. Sweep the tea cup out into the cold where the bus waits. The warm lights show him doubled over behind you laughing and the handsome crowd laughs with him. The water cools on the floor. Try to run to the bus. But you are still undressed. The landlord would not be pleased the floor rotting and wet. Say, you never fixed the stove. This is a cold and vulgar dwelling and you never fixed the window! Take the pen and give her thick skin a good jab. It has been cold in here every night! The bus pulls away. You have missed your chance. The cat races past. What a good long time since the fall.

SIX

Opening

1.

I could begin with this.

My umbrella fluttered.

It tried to fly up and I thought, gravity! That gravity would help hold it.

I thought, let me tell you about my day. First this then this and this. I thought, will this rain never end? Look how it spreads.

I got closer and ran through the doorway. I pulled in my dripping umbrella. A crowd for the elevator. And a wait.

Waiting.

The crowd was not even a crowd but a man two

221

women a child. One old two middle one quite young. Brown hair and light hair and blue eyes brown eyes mouths ears hands. A dark suit and two dresses. And so on. All of us on a ride upward.

I thought, let me tell you about my week. I thought of this. And there was when I this. While the numbers lit and I went up up. There went the man. Let me tell you about my night last night where nothing. A quiet one. Then nothing then nothing then nothing. Let me tell you thank you for the many years. I had never thanked you. For years I stared into my poor knees and fingers. Into the tree tangle past the window.

The woman the woman the child all stepped out. I thought, yes I am so good and fine. I am just so well so thank you. Well enough to handle our last interchange. Well enough to go beyond the interchange. Yes and alone well enough much thanks. One last session and I would offer a gift but I first thought it inappropriate and so I did not act. I thought to offer a present of fruit. Of perfume. A framed picture. But perhaps you should be the one presenting. It would be a fine end to my sitting talking and your sitting looking. A fine end would be for you to extend a gift.

Or perhaps sessions for less cost. But this is the last session hence the present all right. Then perhaps a helpful book you could offer. A kind card or plant.

The pond awaited after. I had planned on tranquillity.

I went one more floor up. A walk through the hall. Another with you. I dragged my umbrella dripping into your office.

2.

I saw into the tangle of trees. Through the clean side of the window through the rain spilling. There through the tangle to the finest tree.

The clock went click   click   click   click.

And on and on. You waited. Looked. Blinked. I am not certain your shoes fit correctly. Your toes seemed wedged unpleasantly. I thought of new ways to shake up the office. A dance. A burst of song. Goodness how the room often narrowed. The walls often pressing. I looked downward. I thought your stare a bit intense at times. For example on this last day as if you were looking for more. Staring when you should have been shouting. Applauding. I thought this day would be different. That there would be a spark of sorts. Fireworks. A cake of sorts but you waited. What could I dredge up for this day? The clock deafened. There must be a story. I drew nothing and spoke of my week while you looked. As always the week. The previous night. The day's walk. Even on this last day the tiresome details of a week. Remember when it was more frenzied? More frantic? We had our goal of sound mind. We went slowly and you leaned in closer. You tried to see inside workings while I tried to break free. I often thought if only to hide deep in the tree tangle. It would have given the finest distance. There in the wonderful outdoors with the world. With the pane of glass between us. The pane clean on your side. I could have sat high in a tree and seen us through sitting. On this last day I tried. With my head I tried to get to the tangle while I gushed. While I poured forth. I opened the window and slid through. Down the brick wall across the wet grass. The rain had stopped. The sky therefore had lightened. To the finest tree in the tangle.

I climbed my legs wrapped tight around the trunk and higher. I squeezed up past a squirrel hole. Past a row of knots. A line of ants. One branch was drenched. One gnarled. One brittle. One held me. How nice in a fine tree seeing. Through the wind. Through the dirty side of the window. To the two chairs. The clock click clicking. And I went on and on. I spilled and you listened and looked and I looked and the sun broke through.

In time gravity pulled me back to my chair.

We sat and I thought had I sat in your chair. I thought this later. Not too later but after. Had I sat there on this last day you would have asked why I chose there to sit. I would have said for years I sat in the other. I would have said for softness. For difference. That I could have seen a different plant. A bus go past and then what? You would have said, and then what? It never ends. A bus.

3.

You walked me to the door and I took my umbrella.

Now what, I know I thought.

There were no gifts.

I ran out so flustered you know. I ran with my head in my fingers so flustered.

Before I set loose for good did we say goodbye? Did we at least shake hands?

4.

The rain restarted spilling heavy. No luck for my umbrella that tried to loosen or was it the wind wanted it? In which case my good luck. I held tight and ran.

To the pond! I thought. There would be time to run around. To celebrate.

You faded into a trace back beyond. We were separated by rain. Signs. Trees. Buses. Then the trace faded.

Under a cover I bought a sunflower. I took a bus ride to the pond.

5.

I see ones with your coat and scuffed shoes. With your face. I stare. I wave my hands. I follow them. They sit in the front of the bus. They stroll by the pond. They crowd through streets. The difference being they do not listen. If they listened I would have stories for them. I would tell them some things I remember. For example some stories which come racing into me at night. Perhaps they would listen but closer anyway they do not resemble. With different coats and faces.

6.

I will explain what I mean on gravity. That what it does is quite sound. Just imagine none is what I mean. That our insides would fly straight to our skulls. Our skulls would toss out to the walls. The walls would fling up to the sky.

7.

If I ever see you on the bus.

I will not sit but stand in the aisle. I will stand by you seated. Hold my arm. We can laugh our heads off. Look at me now so well and fine. Standing here my head could burst so fine. We can laugh hard now.

Look at me fine like you and how curious at last to be so. With a many year goal of fine how curious at last to have reached it. My separate parts are well. My fingers are doing well. My face and knees are fine. My legs feet. The head. Most certainly. Oh there are times. We all have times. You understand. We all have our times. Please nod. Yes we all have times. Please nod yes. Not every day is a sound day. Not every day is firmly rooted. You understand certainly. Please you do. Let go. I move to the back of the bus.

8.

I could have started with the ride to the pond.

That everyone wanted to touch the sunflower. It had a summer face and they wanted to remember the heat. A wind gusted tilting the bus this way and that. The sun shone low and clear below the rain. The pond brightened and I walked to the edge in seeping mud. The sun spread slowly into the pond. A boat in the distance tipped its sail and straightened.

I dug a hole in the mud with my umbrella. I planted the sunflower in the hole. I was loose and free running. The way the wind flipped my umbrella inside out and its sound of birds flapping close. The rain thinned and slowed. I stepped sinking in mud and I should say it was my choosing. Nothing held me I should say. I cut myself loose and stepped the way around the mud with traffic roaring on the highway.

9.

Let me tell the walls my week. I waked. There was toast. Juice. A walk. Then sleep. Then wake. Then sleep.